THE ALL-GIRL, NO-MAN LITTLE DARLIN'S

by Mary Albanese

Oxshott Press

The ALL-GIRL,
NO MAN
LITTLE DARLIN'S

photo Copyright Bob Wade 1979

by MARY ALBANESE

ISBN 978-1-7360234-8-8

For the audio version, the song GATHERING DAISIES was written
by Mary Albanese © 2019. Performed by members of the
Lambertville Acoustic Music Players: Mary Gorman, Bonnie
Berkmeier, Linda Sinclair, Maureen Cruice, and Mary Albanese.

For more information, go to MaryAlbanese.com

Oxshott Press
P.O. Box 718
Neshanic Station, NJ 08853

ACKNOWLEDGEMENTS

Special thanks to the American Women of Surrey Writer's Group, my UK posse of writers, for valuable feedback and support during the birth of this story.

Big thanks go to Bob Wade for creating the image that inspired me to write this story, and to Lisa Wade for allowing its use as the cover of this publication.

I would like to offer a shout-out to the spirit of cowgirls everywhere -- whether they saddle up, create stories or artwork together, harmonize with songs, or just shop in packs. I have been lucky enough to be part of many different groups with a wide-ranging wealth of creative projects, and those bonds never fade but shine on.

CONTENTS

ANABEL MEETS A FOSSIL, 1970

- 1 -

I was twelve years old when I met my Grandma Kline. I'd seen a few pictures of her before, but not many. I knew Dad's parents lived somewhere on the other side of the state, in Pittsburg. They never came to see us and we never went there.

We hardly even talked about them. Sometimes I would hear Mom and Dad mention them in private, but never in happy tones. It's like they were from an old episode from Dad's past but no part of our lives.

Then Grandpa Kline died. My dad went to the funeral by himself. When he came home, he spent a long time talking on the phone with the door shut behind him.

It wasn't until later that I found out why.

I came home from school one day to find Mom all dolled up, with her fire-engine lipstick and best string of pearls.

"We have somewhere to go," She said. "Your outfits are hanging on your doors. Please hurry. Your father doesn't want to be late."

I didn't want to go anywhere, I wanted to watch Nancy Drew. But I knew better than to complain. I went to my room to see the clothes Mom had chosen for me. There was a starchy button-collar shirt and the wool plaid skirt that was itchy on my legs.

I looked at my brother's door. Sammy, who was six, had his

little tweedy suit swinging from a hanger on his doorknob. The suit with the tan shorts. That made me feel better. At least I didn't have to wear sissy pants.

"Why are we getting dressed up for church?" he wailed to Mom standing at the bottom of the stairs. "It's not Sunday. It's only Friday." Then he puffed out his bottom lip.

Mom always thought that looked cute on him.

If I had tried that, I'd have been told to watch out or my face could get stuck that way.

Mom smiled up at my brother. "You've learned the days of the week! Samuel, you look so handsome in your suit. This is your grandmother we're visiting. Your Dad's mother. You want to look your best, don't you?"

"I don't know," he said. "Does she have candy?"

Mom laughed. Sammy was so quick-minded. So clever.

Such a brat.

Out the window, I saw my father down by the car, a scowl etched on his face. That wasn't rare -- he usually looked cross about something. But he was wearing his black suit, the one he wore to weddings and funerals.

I didn't have to guess which event this would be like.

I threw on my clothes and went down to the car before Sammy, taking the seat behind Mom's. That meant more leg room for me.

Sammy came out a minute later, his dimpled knees knocking together in his shorts. "No fair!" he said. "Ana took the good seat."

"Hush up," said Mom, throwing a nervous glance at Dad. "We'll be there soon enough."

That was my second surprise of the day. Mother hardly ever scolded Sammy, her precious. Not even gently.

We didn't talk in the car with Dad driving. We weren't to interrupt his thinking. I figured we were heading to Pittsburgh.

But five minutes later, Dad stopped the car outside a brick

building with a sign -- *The St. Giacomo Retirement Home.* It was so close to our house we could have walked there. On a good day, Sammy and I could fight over the back seat longer than that.

Sammy said, "But we didn't go anywhere!"

"I know it's close," said Mom. "But this was the only facility your father could find. Maybe we can find another place for your grandmother after Christmas, when some of the old folks... go south. In the meantime, this will have to do. We don't want to look all frazzled from walking. First impressions are so important."

"Children," my father said sternly. "You are not to speak unless spoken to. I want you two on your best behavior. We don't want her to get agitated. Your grandmother has always been... unpredictable."

"Yes, Father," Sammy and I said at the same time. But I was confused. What could I possibly say to upset a grown-up? She was like a dinosaur -- a creature from the past who had nothing to do with me.

We went inside the big double doors. I was hit by a blast of air that smelled like rose water and stale laundry. Mom squinched up her nose.

Dad spoke with a lady at the front desk with dark eyebrows that went nearly across her forehead. Her name-tag read: "Miss Belinda."

"Welcome to the best retirement home in the state," she said. "We're number one because we care."

"I'm Ben Kline," said Dad. "My wife and children. This is my son Samuel." Dad never introduced Mom or me with our names, only by how we mattered to him.

"Ah," said Miss Belinda. "You must be here for Maisy Kline. That's what she says to call her. Your mother's room is three doors down on your left. She'll be just thrilled to see you."

At the end of the hall, we entered a stuffy space with pink walls and a row of boxes stacked half-way to the ceiling. In the middle of the room was a Lazy-boy chair with an orange crocheted blanket. Under that blanket was Grandma Kline.

Her skin was saggy and wrinkled. I was sure I'd never let myself look that old.

But the gaze of her eyes was so sharp. Like an eagle that can see for a mile.

"Hello, Ruben," she said to my dad.

"Ben," he said. "People call me Ben."

"I know your name. I gave it to you. Hello, Faith. These are the children?"

"Samuel and Anabel," said my mother. "Samuel is..."

"...six," Grandma Kline cut in. "The girl is twelve. Oh yes. I know what year it is. We have calendars, too."

Mom cleared her throat. "We brought you some tomatoes. I picked them myself. We thought you'd like them."

Mom handed Grandma Kline a paper bag with two red lumps. She took one out and sniffed it. It was splotched with green.

Grandma Kline handed the sack to my brother. "Here, boy. Put these on the window sill for your old grandma. They need to warm up to be sweet."

Sammy dropped the bag on the floor. "Tomatoes aren't sweet. They're sour and they make my tongue sting."

Mother picked up the bag, her face nervous. "Samuel's allergic to them," she said. Actually, what my brother was allergic to was behaving.

"I got to go to the bathroom," Sammy announced.

"Down the hall," said Grandma Kline.

"I'd better go with him," Mom said. She scooted out with Sammy as fast as she could.

Dad looked around. "So, how do you like Philly?"

"How would I know?" said Grandma Kline. "All I've seen is this room."

"Mother, don't start," he said. "I know it wasn't your idea to come here. But I couldn't leave you alone in that house. Not with Dad gone. You know you've never been able to... "

"How would you know?" she said.

Dad grunted, angry and annoyed. She glared back. They locked eyes, like they were having an argument that was so familiar they didn't even need words. My skin prickled, as if the air had turned into poison. I held my breath, trying to make myself as small as I could.

Then Grandma Kline said, "Ruben, there's a kettle in the kitchen down the hall. Why don't you bring us some tea?"

Dad lit out before I could protest. Leaving me...

"Girl!" she barked. "Come closer."

My heart pounded in my chest. Those beady gray eyes stared right through me, as if she was Superman scorching me with her x-ray vision.

I was too scared to move.

"What are you thinking?" she said. "Come on, girl. Don't be shy. Out with it."

All of a sudden, I wasn't nervous anymore -- I was mad. She was not going to turn me into jelly like she'd done with everyone else.

The words just slid out of me. "Why don't you like him?" I told her. "Why doesn't he like you?"

She froze for a few seconds. I thought she'd turn into a witch and zap me with her broomstick. Instead, she leaned back in her chair and sort of relaxed.   "So that's who you are," she said. "Not like your spoiled brother at all." Then I swear, she almost smiled.

Just then Mom and Sammy came back, and Dad too, without the tea. Mom said, "We need to take Samuel home. He's not feeling well."

"Better get him squared away," said my Dad. "We'll be back soon."

He rushed us out of there so fast the door banged my heel.

Behind us, I heard Grandma Kline say, "Bring more tomatoes. You can send them with your girl."

ANABEL'S DILEMMA

- 2 -

I thought Mom and Dad would be ordering me to go back. But a week passed, then another, and I realized no one was going to make me go there again. I had escaped!

But something bothered me. I wasn't worried about the old lady in the stuffy room.

What I couldn't figure out is why she had said what she did. What did she think she knew about me? Mom didn't understand me. She said I was willful and had too many opinions. She said nobody liked a girl who argued so much.

Dad hardly talked to me at all. Samuel was the wonder child – the son he craved -- while I was just stubborn and mouthy.

What could Grandma have figured out about me in that handful of minutes that no one else knew?

Four Fridays later, I was done with school and my homework for the weekend. It was late afternoon. Too early for dinner with nothing but re-runs on tv. I didn't even have a good library book.

Sammy droned on about the new letter he learned. I was getting really tired of hearing him brag.

" 'S' is for snake," he said, dancing in front of the T.V. so I couldn't see it. "It even looks like a snake. It's also for Sammy. I have my own letter. It's the best letter of all. Ana, your name doesn't have an 'S', does it? "

"No, because I'm not a snake."

"Mommm!" he hollered. "Ana called me a name. She says I'm bad like a snake!"

Mother, chopping onions in the kitchen, called out. "Anabel, you know better than to pick on your brother."

Sammy flashed me a grin. I felt like marching right into the kitchen to defend myself.

But why bother? Mom would just take his side. She'd tell me young ladies do not pick fights with their brothers. Young ladies are gracious to young gentlemen.

I grabbed my yellow sweater from the couch and headed out the back door. Just before the screen door banged shut, I called out, "I'm going outside. I'll be back before dinner!"

A MIRROR TO THE PAST

- 3 -

I hadn't actually planned to go see her, my feet just walked me there. So when I found myself standing before her in the pink stuffy room, I didn't have a clue what to say.

After what felt like a very long time, she said, "You have tomatoes?"

I shook my head. "We don't have a garden."

"Ah. The brush-off. I should have known." Then she said, "Your mother's a good liar. I never was. Seems you aren't either."

I wasn't sure if that was a good or a bad thing.

She said, "I'm guessing you're here to find out why your father ignores me."

I shook my head. "I want to know why he ignores *me*."

She looked surprised.

"I try really hard," I told her. "I get good grades in school, but it's never enough. Whatever I do, I just can't please Mom or my Dad. I know that they love me. But sometimes I'm not sure if they like me very much."

She sighed. "You probably ask questions. You probably think about things a great deal."

"Sure, I do."

"That IS the problem," she told me. "Your mother does what your father tells her. But you want to make up your own mind. Some people get itchy when girls think for themselves."

"That doesn't make sense."

"That's how it is," she said. "I found out long ago."

Surely things were different now, I thought. We lived in such modern times, with a man walking on the moon and everything.

She said, "I've been thinking about what you said before. You were right on the money. Your father resents me. He blames me for saddling him with such a rotten father. It's true. Your grandfather was a bully and a pig."

I was shocked speechless. Adults didn't talk that way. They pretended things were fine and would get better, even if they knew they wouldn't.

"Here's one thing I've learned," she said. "It took me a long time to figure it out, and even longer for it to sink in. Maybe if I tell you, you'll be smart enough to catch on sooner."

My head bobbed up and down. I could be smart.

"There's one thing you can't run away from," she told me. "That's yourself. Anabel, you can't escape who you are deep down inside."

"Who is that?" I asked.

She said, "You are someone who gets in trouble for letting your thoughts slip out."

That was true. She'd already seen that.

"You have a quick mind," she added. "But sometimes it's so sharp that people want your words to be softer."

My mouth dropped open. It was like she was reading my report card, reciting my teacher's remarks back to me.

"You're not afraid to disagree," she said, "if you're fighting for something you believe in. Even if everybody else is against you."

"Who told you?" I gasped.

"You did," she said. "You gave it away. Oh, I know exactly who you are."

"How?" I asked.

She thought a moment before answering. "Looking at you is like looking into a mirror. A mirror with a time machine stuck on. I can see it all, the kind of things you're probably fighting right now. What you'll be up against in the future. After all this time, who'd have thought? But I guess genes are like that."

"Like what?"

"Don't you see?" she told me. "You are me, after I've had a few sips of wine. But born fifty years later."

My skin went cold. Could it be true that we were alike, this old fossil and me? Part of me refused to believe it. But another part wondered if that's why I was drawn back.

Her eyes never left me, but her gaze seemed softer now. "You want to ask me something," she said. It wasn't a question. "Go ahead. Whatever it is, I'll do my best to answer."

She didn't seem so scary now. Did she mean it, that she'd talk to me for real, without talking *down* the way adults usually did?

There was only one way to find out.

"If we're so alike," I said, "who are you?"

MAISY'S STORY BEGINS

- 4 -

When you're old, people like to ask, "What's the first thing you remember?" I guess they think if you can't recall what you ate for lunch yesterday, it's because your brain is too full of other things. Important things. Wisdom from long ago.

For most people, if they're honest, they'll say they don't remember which memories came first. Or maybe they'll make something up. Something sentimental. That their first memory is their mother's face, or her gentle voice, lulling them to sleep.

For me, I do remember. But it's not a face or a sound.

It's a smell -- the sticky smell of sweet feed -- oats and corn doused in molasses.

I was born on the prairie in the landmark year of 1900, the start of a brand new century. My Papa ran a feed shop, in the grain barn right behind our house. There, beneath the thick wooden beams, he measured and mixed the grain with his own hands, and the smell of fermenting molasses was everywhere.

Mama couldn't stand the way his clothes reeked of sweet feed, no matter how much lye she soaked them in. She hated his barn coat with the big pockets, the one he didn't let her wash. She hated how that smell became more a part of Papa than his own shadow, that even her fancy perfume, imported all the way from France, couldn't cover up.

But most of all, she hated what it branded her -- a farmer's wife, and me, her one last hope to raise her social standing and get her away from the back roads of Wichita, a farmer's daughter.

It didn't matter that Papa didn't grow the grains himself. In Mama's mind, it was just as bad. He bought from farmers, he sold to ranchers, a fancy word for the same thing. In fact, she thought he was worse than a farmer, because he didn't have land he could have sold off for a ticket back east, to the civilized world of Philadelphia, land of the freedom bell, where Mama was raised and never forgot.

As a small child, I was drawn to that smell of the sweet feed. Papa would often find me out in the granary, asleep on the dirt floor, my little body curled around the base of one of the big wooden bins.

This led to my second oldest memory -- the paddling I got from Mama's wooden spoon for wandering off into *that place* and coming back smelling like my father.

I remember Mama's lessons, too, but that was much later, after Mama took me out of school to sit in the parlor all day long, learning the things that fine ladies were supposed to do. She tried to teach me how to dance with a gentleman, but I stepped on my own feet and knocked into things. I wasn't good at fixing my hair, either, and I hated the whimpering poems Mama drilled into me. Conversation pieces, she called them. Witty little set pieces to charm and impress.

Frankly, I would've rather had dead flies come out my mouth than those silly sonnets, that sometimes didn't even rhyme.

But there was one parlor art I was good at, and that was working thread. My stitches were even and tight, and if it came on a skein and had to be looped, wound, or tied, I could make it into something nice. My clever fingers could knit the thickest yarns, embroider the most fetching designs, and tat plain old cotton thread into a gossamer lace.

I was fast at it, too. Faster than Mama realized, and that's what made it all bearable. Because when Mama took the wagon to town, to buy flour or eggs or a bolt of cloth, I would finish my needlework and head out back.

I knew better than to go to the grain barn, not even for a minute. Mama's nose had a real talent for sniffing that out. But there was a hay barn behind the granary, and for some reason, Mama couldn't tell when I'd been in there.

"What's that smell on you?" she'd say.

"Smell?" I'd ask, all innocent. "I was out in the field, practicing the waltz where I wouldn't knock over the furniture." Then I'd demonstrate, and smack bang into a table or something, and start to cry. Then Mama would rush off to get the rubbing alcohol, forgetting, in her haste, that dried alfalfa didn't smell anything at all like fresh clover.

When I was fifteen, Mama got a message that her sister, back in Philadelphia, was ill. We didn't know what was wrong with my auntie -- only that she was doing poorly, and might not make it without someone on hand to look after her night and day.

I never saw Mama move so fast. In no time at all, she packed up her bag, and one for me, too.

Papa came in from the barn to take Mama to the train station. That's when he saw my bag, packed next to hers.

"Macedonia is coming along, of course," said Mama. She always called me by my full name, all five syllables. Never anything shorter.

Papa shook his head. "Maisy stays here." That's what he called me. They couldn't even agree on my name.

I had never seen him come straight out and challenge Mama before. Mostly, when she'd get in one of her moods and would scold him for his dirty hands or his sweaty clothes, or the fact that she had no culture in her life, he would just hunch into his shoulders and retreat to the grain barn.

But not that day. That day, it seemed like lightning bolts came right out of his eyes. Even Mama couldn't cross him like that. Besides, she was in a hurry to be off. Instead, she hugged me goodbye and had Papa hitch up the wagon to drive her to the station for the next train east.

When Papa returned from town that day, I didn't hear him ride up. I was in the hay shed, with a whole set of dollies I had made out of straw and twine, almost as big as me. We were all sitting together, me and my straw friends, having a party, just for me. Not that it was my birthday. My birthday had passed, without a real party of my own.

Suddenly, the hay shed door swung open on its rusty hinges, letting in a blinding swath of sunlight.

It was my Papa, with his eyes were as dark as a storm. I'd never seen that much anger in him before, and I was afraid. My legs wouldn't move -- they were suddenly as stiff as my friends made from straw.

I remembered what Mama often said, that Papa was uncouth. I didn't know, exactly, what that meant. But I was dead sure I didn't want to find out.

"She's gone," he said. "While she's away, you won't have to hide in here anymore." Then the bitterness left his eyes, and his face turned familiar again. That's when I realized it was Mama he was mad at. Not me.

That summer, for three whole months, I trailed around with Papa. I wore his clothes with the pant legs and sleeves rolled way up, so Mama wouldn't smell the grain on my clothes and know where I'd been. I didn't just go to the granary. I went lots of other places, too. I rode with Papa to the farms, where great seas of pregnant stalks shimmied in the wind. I saw endless rows of upright corn, marching over the hills like soldiers. I paid attention when Papa showed me how to peel back the silky tassels and check for bugs.

And when Papa danced in the fields for the sheer joy of a good crop, to think of the rich, lush feed he would make of it, I was I was right there beside him, whooping and hollering for all I was worth.

Papa taught me the secrets of shucking corn and shearing the kernels in the big iron wheel. He talked to me in a way he never had before, sharing the stories of his life. He told me how he convinced Mama to marry him. How he thought he could make her happy if he did well. If he worked hard and sold good quality grain. But it hadn't worked out that way.

But he told me the good things, too. About the year Bill Cody, who they called Buffalo Bill, brought his show to town. And how Buffalo Bill walked right into our grain barn, shook hands with my Papa, and said it was the best feed he'd ever seen.

Papa met all of Bill's friends, too. He smoked a pipe with Sitting Bull, and traded stories with Pawnee Bill way before he became a legend, himself. Papa smiled when he talked about Frank Butler and Annie Oakley, and the way she shot a cigarette out of a man's teeth at 20 paces. I heard how he'd seen another woman, no bigger than Mama, crack a lasso into the air that could bring down a raging bull.

As I listened, enthralled, I matched Papa step for step, shovel for shovel. I kept pace with him, but not like a youngster. Not like a girl.

Like a partner.

Then when night came, and I fell onto my goose feather quilt too tired to pull it over me, I knew I'd never been so sore. Or so gritty.

Or so thankful for my life.

But it couldn't go on forever. My carefree days with Papa were numbered and would have to end.

It wasn't the only letter we got from Mama that summer, rancid with her perfume. But it was the only one that mattered.

"Your auntie's recovered," said Papa, his face pale as he looked up from that single folded sheet. "Your Mama's train gets in the day after tomorrow."

I still had two days! I said, "That's enough to get that shipment off for the Parker Brothers."

Papa shook his head. "I'll take care of the shipment. You need to get cleaned up for your Mama. You know how she is."

There was no arguing with him, no more talking at all. Because once the specter of Mama was upon him, he slid back into himself, stooping his shoulders. And shutting me out.

He was right about one thing. It did take me two days in hot suds to soften the sun-baked cracks in my skin, and turn back into the clean little lady I'd been when Mama left. So when Mama returned, gushing with tales from her trip, where the ladies wore hats with feathers and everything was so grand, she thought our lives would go on just like before.

But some things had changed.

Fueled by her trip, Mama became relentless, scolding Papa to his face now for all the things that he wasn't. At those times, he would trudge off to the granary, ignoring her words. He'd ignore me, too, when I tried to catch his eye, to tell him I understood. He didn't see me anymore, wouldn't even look at me, as if we were strangers. As if the summer never happened.

I had changed, too. Because I'd seen how it could be, and had been treated like I mattered. After that, even sneaking off to the hay barn with my straw people no longer seemed exciting. It just felt empty.

I thought with time, Mama's zeal would fade. But I was wrong. As the days went on, it only got stronger. She kept up with her letters, and wrote to her sister's neighbor, who had a son just a few years older than me. Mama said it was a good match, and I should be thankful the neighbor was willing to have me, sight-unseen, as her daughter-in-law.

I told Papa straight away, thinking he'd come to my rescue. That he wouldn't let Mama marry me off to some city boy I'd never met. I thought he'd put his foot down again, just like before.

But he didn't. He said I was growing up, and he couldn't stop it. That it was wrong to even try. And maybe Mama was right. Maybe he didn't have the right to hold me back from the kind of life that a lady should have. Then he dipped his head, turned his back, and headed out to the grain barn. At that moment, for the first time ever, I understood how Mama could get so mad at him.

But I couldn't stay mad long. I wasn't about to give up on him, either. I had to win him back. I had to make him care about me again. I had to impress him -- show him I was worth fighting for.

I went to the hay shed to think. There were the familiar bales of hay, some stacked, some loose, cinched with the rough baling twine.

I cut off some loops of twine, and laid them out in a line. Then I sliced off the knots, and braided the strands into the smoothest rope I could make. It wasn't hard to do, it was like working with big thread, and I could do that just fine.

I chain-braided my rope with a slip knot at the end. Not tied onto the end, the way knots are usually done, my slip knots were woven right into the fabric of the rope. That made them clean and strong, and if those knots landed smack onto whatever I was aiming for, I could flick my hand and the knot would grab hold and practically tie itself.

Every second I could leave Mama's watchful eye, I practiced throwing rope. I escaped to the hay shed and lassoed my straw people. When they'd been squeezed into shreds, I made smaller targets. Then smaller ones still, until I was so accurate with my rope, I could and snatch a small bunch of straw with a loop thrown from 20 paces away.

I figured this was good. But was it good enough? What if Papa didn't care anymore? What if all his stories of working hard, and doing your best, and being proud of your work -- what if he only meant that for himself, and he didn't believe it of me?

So I didn't tell him right away. I found plenty of excuses not to. As the weeks dragged on, with Mama talking about her plans, and Papa ignoring us both, I practiced in secret with my rope, waiting for the best time to show him.

Then one night he didn't come in for dinner. That wasn't unusual. He didn't come in for bedtime, either, which had also happened before.

But when he hadn't come in by morning, and breakfast had come and gone, Mama sent me out to the grain barn to fetch him.

I found him all right. Not far from where Bill Cody shook his hand, in the same place he used to find me as a toddler. By the big grain bin, folded over on the ground.

But Papa wasn't asleep.

The doctor said it was his heart, that Papa must have strained it. Pushed it too far.

I think he just let go. I think he lost the heart for living. Mama always said there no dignity in running a common grain shop. Maybe he finally believed her.

Next thing I knew, the preacher came. Then the neighbors. After them came the lawyers and the bankers with their fancy suits, and their hungry eyes, eager to buy us out.

Mama was surprised to find out what the business was worth. All that money, she said, from a smelly, dirty feed shop like that? Well, what do you know, she told me. Papa had done one right thing after all. With all that money, she didn't have to wait until I was sixteen. We could move right away. We could go to Philadelphia, and wear crinkly skirts, and sit for hours at orchestra concerts and dinners and fashionable parties. With all of that, she said I would charm Auntie's neighbor boy for sure.

My chest went numb, like the rest of me. My head felt so heavy I could hardly see. That night, after the bankers and the lawyers left, I buried in the folds of my goose feather quilt, hoping I'd never have to come out.

But late in the blackness of night, I work to the screech-owl, my body bathed in a horrible sweat.

I wheezed for breath. The air was hot and thick. And sticky. Sticky with the smell of sweet-feed.

I heard a voice, not my own, shouting in my head.

Run.

I slipped out the house and went to my hay shed. There, feeding herself since no one else was doing it, was one of Papa's horses. She was a spit-white horse with big dark spots. Papa had got her on a trade. A bum trade, Mama had said, because Spackles wasn't any good as a cart horse. She was too nervous for that -- didn't trust humans enough.

Mama also didn't approve of the horse's color. She'd said it wasn't a clean shade like a thoroughbred, or even a half-bred. No, indeed. Spackles was splotched like a common Indian pony -- like stains on a blouse. I guess the bankers didn't want her, either, because they'd left her by herself, away from the proper wagon stock tied up in the barn.

I looped my rope around Spackles' neck to walk her back to the stables. I meant to put her in the stalls with the other horses.

But I saw my father's saddle, and some of his clothes hanging on a peg.

In my mind, I heard that voice again, so much like Papa's, pounding inside my brain.

Run.

I knew that would be foolish. No thinking person would have considered it. Horses are afraid in the dark, and Spackles was green-broke and skittish even in the best of conditions.

I was surely no expert rider. I'd spent three months on the back of Papa's saddle, just hanging on.

But I was past thinking about that.

I don't know if it was really Papa's ghost that told me to go. Or if it was my own voice, stifled for so long, but finally set loose.

All I know is that I pulled on Papa's clothes, his pants and his barn coat with the big pockets.

Then I climbed into that saddle and smacked Spackles' rump as hard as I could, forced to cling for dear life on that crazed, panicked horse.

It was reckless and dangerous, I knew these things. I knew the night was likely to end with me thrown onto the ground, my back or my legs broken. If not my neck.

But it was too late for regrets.

Whatever would happen was already in motion.

INTO THE NIGHT

- 5 -

My heart pounded in my chest as Spackles ran hard. I didn't try to steer her, I didn't have a plan. She knocked against trees trying to scrape me off, but I hung on tight, my hands locked in a death-grip around the saddle horn.

After a while, my limbs bruised from being banged around, I lost track of time. Spackles got tired and slowed her insane pace. It felt like a dream as we jostled along in the black sea of night.

Then, strangely, the stars started to fade, washed out by the dawn -- and I was still on her! The world became real again. I could see trees, and dirt below me, and spring shoots rising up from the ground.

Spackles stopped at a creek with a stand of trees off to the side. I climbed down and watched her drink. With some stalks I made a nest for myself in the weeds by the bank. It was spring and the air was sharp. I yearned for my goose feather quilt back home on my bed, and thought of the eggs Mama would be making, sizzling in bacon fat on her black skillet. My stomach twisted at the thought of it.

That's when I made a deal with myself. I could go back or I could go on. It wouldn't serve to mix the two. Once I banished thoughts of home, sleep came easy. Some hours later, with the sun shining down, I woke with a jump to find myself there, in this strange patch of thick woods with no walls and no roof. I saw Spackles nearby, nibbling on the new spring sprigs, and it came to me that this place wasn't so strange after all. It was the same sun I knew. The same air. And there was nothing odd about watching a horse eating brush.

It's what Spackles did best.

The creek was cold and clear, just like the water in our well, and it tasted sweet on my dry lips. That's when I realized that this place felt more right for me than Mama's fancy parlour with her stiff dresses and her rules.

But I knew Mama would send people out looking for me. I was not of age yet to make my own choices. If they caught me, I'd be off to the city, bundled up like a blanket for sale to the richest boy Mama could find.

The wind picked up and funneled through the draw of the creek. I strained to hear if it carried voices with it. *Maisy... Maisy...* Was it the rustling of the weeds, or were they already coming for me?

The sounds didn't seem to get closer so I stayed where I was. It was a good spot I picked, with Spackles shadowed in the trees.

I knew I'd slept a long time, and figured from the sun angle we had a good several more hours before dark. Then we could move on again.

I tried to go back to sleep but couldn't. I'd never gone without a meal before, and my stomach hurt from growling so much. I dug around in the pockets of Papa's coat, but there was no food in them. Just some papers and pictures -- no help at all.

I had never in my whole life been this hungry before, and I wondered if I might just fall over and die from starvation.

Still, it was better than going back.

The saddle pad under Papa's saddle was a thin square of flannel. I laid it out and filled it with grain tufts peeled from the tops of the tough creek grass. For this day and the next, at least Spackles would eat well.

By late afternoon, my face stung from the wind and the sun. I picked some long stalks around me, empty now of their seed pods, and started to weave. By the time the sun went down, I had a lopsided sort of a hat.

From then on, I traveled at night, sleeping by day tucked into some gully or behind an old shed. When the sun dropped into the far plains, I followed it as straight as I could, in a line heading west.

Spackles didn't like carrying me at night, but she did so, grudgingly, because I knew where to find the best scrub grass. She didn't like carrying me in the daytime, either. In fact, she didn't like me at all, and reminded me of that as often as she could with the disgusted way she rolled her eyes.

For me, I foraged berries and food-weeds. That kept me from starving. But I needed protein, and found it in the raw eggs I raided from chicken coops. At first I was clumsy at it, but soon learned how to do it right, clucking like a big hen to trick the roosters so they wouldn't squawk in alarm.

It was stealing, and I wasn't pleased about that, but there wasn't much else I could do about it. Most times, I would leave a little something in exchange for the eggs, like a little basket woven from grass. My weaving quickly improved, and in no time at all, I had myself a straw hat as fine as anything bought from a store. I also made a sleeping mat, and woven pouches I tied to my saddle to hold my supplies. I imagined the farmer's wife as she went to the hen-house, and her surprise to find a perfectly-shaped basket, just right for her chores, exactly where the eggs should have been. It was as fair a trade as I could make, and I hoped if I got caught, maybe they'd go easy on me.

I continued west, looping around the towns, dipping into the farms on the outskirts. I passed Garden City, Lamar, Pueblo, Salida and went over Monarch Pass -- 1,000 feet high -- before riding down into the Black Canyon.

After weeks travelling like this, I found The Rockies now to my back, like a wall of church spires between me and the prairie. I figured I must have turned 16 by now, which made me legal in most states.

It made me feel brave, ready to take a chance. Besides, I was awfully sick of raw eggs.

I slipped into Grand Junction one night, half-expecting to see my picture tacked up all over town: *Thieving Egg Girl Wanted for Society Matrimonial.*

There were wanted posters, all right. Snarling faces of bandidos, nailed to the shop doors. Those pictures used to scare me. But now, they seemed like my allies. With such desperados on the loose, who would care about me?

The town was quiet, mostly. Except for one little patch of noise where a piano played a raucous honky-tonk tune.

I followed the sound into a saloon. I slipped in and was immediately assaulted by the smell of cigar smoke and whiskey. It was too loud and too bright, but I watched from the shadows and listened and learned what I needed to know.

The next morning as the town woke up, I made my way to the tailor shop three blocks past the saloon. I found the tailor all right. He was tall and perfectly scrubbed, from the top of his bald head to his shiny shoes. I'd never seen a man before with fingernails as clean as a newborn child. After all those days on my own, I was so tongue-tied, I could barely get the words out. Of course he had no interest in hiring me, smelling like sage and stale horse sweat.

I started to leave town, already planning my next chicken coop raid, when the scent of frying sausage hit me so hard I went weak in the knees. I followed my nose to a hotel and rang the bell. A stout woman appeared in a grease-stained apron.

"Can I help you?" she asked.

"I'll do your mending for a plate of that sausage."

"You can mend?" she said. "Are you any good?"

I started to laugh. I don't know why. I guess it just felt good that she didn't say no right away. Or maybe it just felt strange, talking to someone who didn't treat me with distain the way Spackles did.

I showed her what I could do. I took her apron and hemmed a frayed patch on the edge. Then I embroidered daisies on the stains, so that it looked like they belonged there, like part of the design.

In return, she gave me a plate of sausage and a hot bath. She told her friends and they brought me their mending, too. They asked where I came from, and I said I just drifted in with the wind. Which was more or less true, and they didn't ask to hear more. When I'd finished patching all their natty clothes, the hotel lady pointed me north where her sister-in-law lived with four kids sprouting out of their clothes. I was no longer a runaway or a chicken egg thief. I was *that drifter girl who could mend*.

When I left town about two weeks later, I had a tidy roll of salt beef, a wool blanket, and a couple of coins. I felt like a queen.

LILL'S BIG DREAM

- 6 -

I sewed my way north, through Rifle, Craig, and Baggs. Sometimes I had the name of someone to look up. Somebody's sister or cousin. If not, hotels were my best bet. The folks that ran them were thrifty and busy, with little time for their own mending. Besides, they knew everyone in town. They knew exactly whose spring coat was in tatters or their socks full of holes.

I cut over to Rock Springs where a woman with a brand new baby asked me to stay on, to mind her three older children. They weren't bad kids, and it meant a roof over my head and meals twice a day. But it was still summer, with days long and warm, and new towns just over the hill. I wasn't quite ready to trade in my saddle sores.

So I went on, my saddle basket now full of needles and pins, jingling on the back of Spackles' saddle like little bells.

Just south of Jackson, Spackles slipped on a rock and her right front hoof splintered. We hobbled to town, with her leaning on my shoulder and making faces the whole way, annoyed that despite all the time she carried me, when her leg went bum, I wasn't able to do the same for her.

I spotted a hotel just as we got into town. It smelled like fresh bread rising in the oven. I could often get a slice of bread free, just for complimenting the cook. But I passed it by, for Spackles' sake.

In the middle of town, right in the center, there was a proper town square marked by four pillars of antlers. Right in the center, in place of pride, was a saloon. I pushed through the swinging doors and made my way to the counter.

There was a girl there, not much older than me, with a smile as wide as the sky.

"Howdy there," she said, smacking down a glass in front of me. "What's your pleasure?"

"I don't need a drink," I said. "My horse shot her hoof. She can hardly walk. Who do I need to see?"

"There's Justin Banks," she said. "He does most of the big jobs around here."

"I can't pay much," I said. "Only in trade."

Her eyes twinkled. "Then you want to see Rosey."

"Who's that?" I asked. "Can she fix my horse?"

"If she can't, nobody can. Come on. I'll take you there."

I looked around. The place wasn't full, but it wasn't empty, either. At the center table there were three scruffy fellows with beards shot with gray. They'd be wanting more drinks, for sure.

"Who's going to tend the bar?" I asked.

"I do what I please," she said. "And to tell the truth, I was getting bored in here anyway. But first, you look thirsty."

She filled my glass with water from a copper dipper. It was cold and clean with a metallic zing, and it felt good going down. Then she stepped out from behind the counter.

She must have been standing on a stool back there, because when she came out, I could see she was just a little thing. Full grown, but she barely up to my neck, and I wasn't that tall myself. She wore these huge fur chaps strapped over her pants, black bear I think, that made her look as wide as she was tall. She was proud of those chaps, you could see it by the way she swaggered in them -- not so much a walk or a stride, but a forward-rolling side-step.

"Some people just don't want to hire a woman," she said. "That's why."

Why, what, I wondered, still staring at her fuzzy pants.

"But don't worry," she went on. "Rosey's a fine farrier."

Now I was really confused. "My pants are just fine," I said. "I don't need any fur on them. I just need a hoofer. For my horse's foot."

She laughed. "A farrier is a hoofer. Don't you know nothing about horses?"

"Not really," I said. "All I know is to point them where I want to go and to hang on."

She laughed again. "I'm Lill. And we ain't had nobody like you pass through here in a long time."

I didn't know if this was a compliment or not.

We went outside and I showed her Spackles, tied to a post nearby.

Lill's eyes lit up. "Your horse is something else."

"My horse is a lazy nag with a bum leg."

She laughed again. Apparently, the whole world was one big joke to this girl.

She looked across the street, nodding towards a black horse with a Mexican saddle with lots of trim work and silver buckles polished up bright. The horse was leaning against a fence post, itching his right flank. A pair of fine ladies were walking by carrying parasols, and as the black horse saw them, he snapped to attention. He puffed out his chest, big and proud as they went by, admiring his musculature. I could hardly believe it, that a horse could care what people thought of him. Spackles surely didn't.

Lill chuckled. "That's my Thunder," she said. "He is pretty and don't he know it."

Spackles snorted impatiently. "Easy, girl," I said. "I haven't forgotten about your foot." I patted her side while Lill crossed the street to her black horse.

"Walk your horse and follow me," she said. "Thunder and I will show you the way. Don't worry. We'll go slow so you can follow."

With that, she took off like a bullet. I watched her ride out of view, her furry chaps flapping against the black horse like they were wings. They might as well have been, the way they flew away.

I leaned into Spackles to give her my shoulder and followed as best I could. I couldn't see Thunder's tracks, but he did leave a dust trail.

Just when I thought we'd lost them, I'd see Lill in the distance, waving her arm in the air, then blasting off again on that proud black horse.

We finally caught up with them just outside of town. Thunder was tied out for grazing, while Lill sat on a stump in front of a cabin. It was made out of logs with a barn door thrown open wide, with tools lined up on the walls all neat and tidy. Behind it was a smaller shack, much less fussed over. A sleeping shack, it looked like, for someone who spent more time on their work.

I could see Lill talking to a big fellow, his back to us, wearing clompy boots and a leather-hide apron around his hips. Exactly the kind of gear you wear to shoe horses.

I felt like I'd been had. I had eaten a lot of Lill's dust to be led to the town's farrier *man* -- to the fellow I couldn't afford.

But when 'he' turned around, I saw my mistake. 'He' was a she -- a man-shouldered woman with a handshake that could choke a chicken.

"How do," she said. "I'm Rosey, and I hear you got a horse that needs fixing, but no money to pay. Is that about it?"

"Just about," I said. "I'm Maisy. Nice to meet you. And I have some money, but I'd rather pay in trade. I can..."

"Not now," said Rosey. "We'll deal with the horse first." She lifted up Spackles' front leg, then shook her head in disgust. "Jiminy, you let this poor thing walk on this?"

I shrugged. Was there another choice?

"Can you fix it, Rosey?" asked Lill. "You got to. You just got to. 'Cause you see, Maisy and me are going on up to Cody. We're going to join Buffalo Bill and his Wild West Show. I'm going to tear around the ring on Thunder. You know he's only got one speed -- fast.

And I've been thinking how fine it would be to have someone to go with. And along comes Maisy here, and... Maisy, what can you do, anyhow?"

"What?" I said. "I never said all that. Why would I come all the way here, across the Rockies, to join up with Buffalo Bill?"

"What else you going to do, heading north?" said Lill. "Except for Old Bill, who just happens to be the most famous person in the whole world, there ain't nothing north of here but winter. Besides, you got this fine show horse. Look at her big bright spots. People will see those from the far side of the ring."

"Just ignore her," said Rosey. "Lill's been talking like this since March, ever since she shot that bear and had those chaps made, trying to hoodwink somebody to go to Cody with her."

I looked at Spackles. It was the first time I'd heard anyone call her a fine anything.

I didn't think I had a plan. But could Lill be right? After all, I had come a long way, always heading west. Did I have a plan so secret I hadn't even told myself?

"My papa knew Buffalo Bill Cody," I said. "He was his grainier a long time ago."

"I knew it!" said Lill. "So, what'cha gonna do for Bill? To make yourself part of the show?"

Rosey shook her head. Then she picked up a long iron file and started to shave the frayed bits from Spackles' hoof. As I watched the filings peel off, I thought about Lill's question. What could I do? Did Old Bill need some mending? Were there costumes to make, fringed leather with beads?

I looked at Spackles, trying to see her as something fancier than a beast with a bad attitude clipped to a post with a piece of baling twine -- not even properly fastened but tied with a slip knot looped into the end.

Of course. It came out of my mouth before I could stop it.

"I can throw a rope."

Rosey sniffed. "Shoot, anybody can throw a rope."

"Not like me," I said. "I catch things with it. I'm pretty good at it. At least I used to be."

"Can you catch a cow?" Lill asked. "Like a raging bull with crazy-wild eyes?"

"I never tried that. I'd have to see."

"We'll all see!" said Lill clapping her hands with excitement. "Rosey, you remember that mad steer with Deek Runyan? The one he wanted to brand?"

"Sure," said Rosey. "He said he'd pay double if I could get an iron on that thing's hide."

"Here's your chance," said Lill.

Rosey didn't say anything. She just kept filing Spackles' hoof, then smeared the gaps with a gray paste that smelled like beaver musk. Finally, she wrapped the whole thing in white sticky-cloth.

"No riding this horse for three days," Rosey told me. "In the meantime, you can stay with me and do chores to earn your keep. And your first job is, let's go catch us that steer."

ANABEL WANTS MORE

- 7 -

All of a sudden Grandma stopped talking. I realized I was standing there, with my boring kid's life, in a musty pink room that smelled like chlorox. My legs felt stiff and heavy -- they'd fallen asleep as I stood there.

"What happened?" I asked. "You can't stop now. Did you rope that bull? Did Rosey brand it?"

She nodded at the wall clock. "It's late. I expect your mother will be making your dinner."

She was right. I couldn't believe it was almost six o'clock.

"Just a little bit more," I begged her. "I can get home really fast."

"I've talked enough for one day," she said. "And you need to get home."

"Please, just one little question," I said. "Did you become a real live cowgirl?"

She didn't answer, but for the first time since I'd met her, her face lit up with a smile.

I said, "Why didn't my father tell me any of this?"

She shrugged. "He doesn't know." I could hardly believe that. "Abner, my husband," she explained, "sent your father off with nurse maids as soon as he was born. Then it was boarding school. My husband didn't want me to have anything of my own."

"You never told Dad?" I asked her. Then I wished that I hadn't, because every wrinkle on her face turned sad.

"I thought I might finally have the chance, with Abner gone. I thought we could start over. But some things you can't undo. I'm afraid it's just too late for your father and me."

"Can I come back next Friday?" I asked. "I get off school early on Fridays."

Her eyes twinkled. "If you want to waste your time with an old fool like me, I guess I can't stop you."

"You won't forget where you left off?"

"No, ma'am," she said. "I don't ever forget."

I ran all the way home. I jogged in through the back door just in time to help Mom set the table. She didn't seem to notice I'd been gone.

I didn't tell her. I didn't tell Dad or Sammy or anyone else. It made me feel special, to have such a secret.

The weekend came and went. I started a new week at school and did my chores and my homework without even a grumble. I rushed to get everything done and out of the way.

In the meantime, I checked the fridge for tomatoes. I hid the best one in the very back. I hoped she would like it. Besides, if I got caught going to visit her, it would give me an excuse. After all, Dad had sort of almost agreed.

Those next six days were long, but in a way, kind of exciting. I would be doing something normal -- taking a quiz or putting out the trash, and I'd remember. It gave me a tingly feeling deep inside to know I knew something that no one else did.

I had an adult on my side. Not just a regular old adult, but a real live rodeo star of the wild, wild west. And out of everyone in the whole world, I was the only one who was going to get to hear all about it.

MAISY'S STORY CONTINUES

- 8 -

Rosey hitched up her wagon to the biggest horse I'd ever seen. His name was Big Red, and with his coat the color of a new brick, he was surely both of those things. With Rosey and I in the wagon, and Lill on black Thunder, we rode off to Runyan's farm to find that wild steer.

Runyans was a good sized spread with a split log fence and a respectable herd of cattle. Most of them clustered in one corner of the pasture except for one bull that stood all by himself. I could see by the way he jerked his head around that he was *the one.*

Rosey lit a charcoal fire and heated her irons until they glowed red. Then Lill and Thunder and I went in through the gate.

"I'll chase him towards you," said Lill from on top of her horse. "Be ready with your rope."

I checked my knot. It was ready to go.

That bull was wild, all right. But he was smart, too, because he could see I wasn't on a horse. To charge past us, all he had to do was go through me.

I gulped down my fear -- no time for that -- and threw my rope. It landed wide.

I snapped it back to me, and threw it again.

This time it fell short.

The bull came on, pounding the ground with his hooves as he barreled straight towards me.

It was him or me. I would only get one more toss before I was gored by his horns.

I caught a glimpse of Lill on her black horse. She was laughing her head off.

I raised my rope high, twirling the loop, watching how the wind fed it.

Then I looked into that bull's eyes. Watching his hooves, how fast they were ploughing the ground, how straight he came at me, not a whiff to either side.

This was it. Strike three and you're out.

I let the loop fly. It snaked away from me and sailed over that bull's horns, then down onto his thick meaty neck. Once it was there, his own momentum tightened the knot.

He snorted and bellowed, angry to have this rope choking his windpipe.

It was a thrilling moment, my first live catch.

But it hadn't made him slow down. He was still charging towards me, but now with a score to settle. I was attached to this mad crazy bull, who came closer every second, with no idea how to stop the collision.

From nowhere, Lill charged up on Thunder. "Give me your rope," she said.

I threw my end of the rope at her and she caught it out of the air. She tossed me another rope, then with her piece of rope still tied to the bull, she ran a circle around it.

The bull stopped in his tracks, flaring and fuming, not sure who he should charge. He threw down his horns and bucked like a horse.

Rosey called out from the side. "Lasso his feet while his back legs are up."

"I can't," I called back.

"What do you mean, you can't? You caught him before."

"That was with *my* rope. I can't do it with yours."

"Hell and tarnation!"

Oh, she was mad -- nearly as mad as that bull. With her branding irons under her arm, Rosey stomped up to that bull. She grabbed his horns, and with the sheer force of her anger, she snapped his head to the side and powered him to the ground. Once he was down she tied his legs. In no time at all she had that bull trussed up as tidy as a Christmas package done up with a bow.

I watched as Rosey singed an "R" into the bull's hide.

Lill came up on Thunder, cackling so hard I thought she'd fall off.

"The look on your faces," she said. "Both of you. What a pair!"

Once Rosey had finished her branding, she cut the bull free. She didn't ask if she could cut my rope. She just did it. The bull whipped to his feet and ran off, squealing like a pig. Then Rosey turned to me.

"So, my rope's not good enough for you?" she said.

"It's not that," I said. "My rope has a special knot. It had, anyways, before you cut if off. I made this rope with the knot it in. It's the only kind of knot I can throw. I don't know how to throw a rope with a regular knot."

"Who cares?" said Lill. "Maisy, you roped that bull, clean as could be. And Rosey, you got right in there and wrastled it to the ground. I didn't know you could do that."

"You think every critter I brand just sits still for me?" Rosey snarled.

"What I think," said Lill, "is that you should come along with Maisy and me and star with us in Buffalo Bill's wild west show."

"You're as crazy as that bull," said Rosey. "I have a shop and a house that are all mine. I built them myself, with my own two hands. And you want me to give that up? To go traipsing up to Cody to chase after your dream?"

"Suit yourself," said Lill. "But you'd be great. We'd all be great. Heck, we are great. All three of us. Even if you don't come along."

We found Deek Runyan and gave him the news. He was

mighty impressed we took care of his bull, and paid Rosey what was her due. Then, since we'd helped, Rosey took us all out for a good meal and a drink. She insisted she had money to burn, and that, I was about to find out, was another thing Rosey did very well.

*

We had a fine meal in town, a rich beef stew dunked with sourdough bread, so moist and tasty it practically jumped down my throat. After that, Rosey offered to take us out for a drink. Lill wasn't too keen on the idea, but Rosey insisted and got her way.

We went back to the same saloon where Lill worked. There were the same three fellows at the middle table, with two more with them that were just as scraggly. At the bar was a portly man with a black mustache. He wasn't too happy to see Lill.

"Guess what, Boss?" she said, pretending to ignore the steam coming out of his eyes.

"You let me down again," he said. "That's what. How many times have I told you not to leave your station like that? With customers needing a drink and everything. And who knows what could have happened, with nobody watching the cash box? Good thing it was just the Hjodaddy brothers in here or we could have been robbed blind."

The fellows at the table looked surprised, or maybe annoyed that they hadn't thought of it themselves.

"Come off it," said Lill. "Ain't nobody but those Hjodaddies ever comes here in the middle of the day."

"That is the truth," said one of the Hjodaddies scratching his stubbly chin. "I was just taking a little break," Lill told her boss. "That's all it was. But I'm back, Pete. See?"

"I'll say you're taking a break. A permanent break. You're fired, Lillith Geller."

"Too late. I quit," she shot back. "I'm gonna be a star. And then you'll be sorry that you fired a star. A real hero of the American west."

"You finally found somebody to go north with?" asked a different Hjodaddy brother, picking something out of his hair.

"Yes, sir, I did," said Lill. "And we're here to celebrate. I'd like a mint julep, Pete. I'm a customer, now. And Rosey's paying."

"I'm not paying for some girlie drink like that," said Rosey, stepping up to the bar. "Whiskey, Pete. I'll take three. For me and my friends."

Lill frowned as Rosey got the drinks and took them to the table furthest in the back. We sat down with her. Rosey drank her shot and Lill's. I sniffed at mine, stuck my tongue in for a taste, but it stung my throat like I'd swallowed a handful of bees.

"You could use this for lamp fuel," I said.

Rosey laughed and drank mine, too.

Lill sat there, her big eyes watching. And for the first time, she was not laughing at all.

Then Lill said, "I think we should leave. Come on, Rosey. Let's just go."

Rosey hauled herself up from her chair. "If you're not going to drink or be sociable, I'll just go sit with the brothers."

"Fine," said Lill. "Be that way."

Rosey got up and strolled over to the table in the middle of the room. The Hjodaddies had their sleeves rolled up for arm-wrestling. When they saw Rosey come over, they pulled up a chair.

Lill frowned.

I waited for her to say something, but she just sat there, all worried.

"Sorry about your job," I said.

Lill shook her head. "That ain't it. It's just that this isn't good for Rosey to start in like this. It's why people don't pay her. Not that she isn't good at shoeing and that. They just don't want to see her do it to herself."

I looked over at Rosey, her elbow on the top end of an arm-wrestling match. "She looks like she's doing just fine to me."

"Maybe so," said Lill. Then a little corner of her smile came back and we talked a while.

Lill told me about all the different jobs she'd worked in town. It seemed like she'd worked an awful lot of different jobs for someone not much older than me. And I told her about some of the places I'd come through. She didn't ask me why I went from town to town, and I didn't ask why she had to leave so many jobs. It just seemed better that way.

All of a sudden, the Hjodaddy closest to Rosey tossed a hand of cards in the air and started to cheer. "I got me a house!" he said. "We don't have to sleep in the barn no more!"

"You don't have my house for long," said Rosey. "I'm fixing to win it back with my next hand." Then she hollered out. "Bartender, give us another round. I'm feeling lucky."

"This is what I was afraid of," said Lill. She got up from her seat and marched up to the bar, her furry chaps banging into the empty tables on the way.

"Pete," she said. "Cut Rosey off. She's had more than enough."

Pete shook his head. "In this place, you don't get to say who can have a drink and who can't. Remember, Lill? You don't work here no more."

As if to spite her, he took a whole tray of drinks over to Rosey.

Lill grabbed my arm. "Maisy, this is the second house Rosey's lost like this. You got to do something. Before it gets worse."

"Me?" I said. "What am I supposed to do?"

"Rope her," said Lill. "If her hands are tied up, she can't gamble no more. Come on, Maisy. You can do it. She wouldn't be nearly so hard to catch as that steer."

I couldn't believe Lill was serious, that she really expected me to lasso a real person, and hog tie her up, right there in front of everyone.

"I can't," I said. "I... I don't have my rope. Besides, Rosey cut the knot off."

"There's rope in her wagon," said Lill. "You can make another knot. It don't have to be great. It's not like you have to throw it that far. All you got to do is slip it over her head."

The whole thing was crazy. But then, again, I looked over at Rosey, smiling like a fool despite losing her house, and the Hjodaddy brothers closing around like a pack of dirty wolves.

"Okay," I said. "Let's get the rope."

By the time we got it from the wagon and came back in, the Hjodaddies were hooting. "I always wanted my own workshop," said one of the taller ones. "And now I got it! All I need now is a wagon and a big old horse to pull it. Come on, Rosey. Care to go double?"

"Quick!" said Lill. "Before she gives it all away. It would just about kill her, to lose Big Red."

That's when I did it. I bent the rope double, then fed the end through the loop to make the quickest slider knot I could. I flung it over Rosey's head and wriggled it down her, letting it take hold just below her shoulders. I handed Lill one strand and held onto the other. Between the two of us, we dragged her towards the door.

As we did, Lill grinned at me, her smile back on. "Told you," she said. "Catching a drunk is a whole heck of a lot easier than roping a bull."

"Hey!" said one of the Hjodaddies. "You can't just stop a game right in the middle of the action."

"Shut up," said Lill. "Didn't you get enough of her, Joe, or Jule, or whatever the hell your name is?" Then she turned towards Pete. "And as for you, I'm *glad* I don't work for you no more. Tempting Rosie like that."

Then she called Pete a gutless son of a gun and a few other

names besides, which I guess he deserved for the way he let Rosey get rolled by those Hjodaddy brothers.

Out front, we dragged Rosey to the wagon and loaded her into the back. She didn't have no more fight in her, stumbling around.

Lill vaulted onto Thunder's back. "You drive the wagon," she said. "Meet me at Rosey's house."

"You mean she didn't really lose it?" I said. "The bet didn't count, because she was drunk?"

"Of course it counts," said Lill. "But I didn't hear them say nothing about her stuff. We got to save what we can, before they get there."

*

I'd never driven a wagon before. But it was easier than riding a horse. At least it was harder to fall off. And Big Red knew his way home.

We got to Rosey's place and ransacked it, mostly the shop, loading as many of her tools that would fit into the wagon beside her. She wasn't any help, passed out in the back and snoring away. Lill and I kept loading until we heard singing coming down the street -- a warbling five-part harmony. A victory song. I grabbed one last load of blankets from the house, tied Spackles to the back of the wagon, and drove it off just before they got to us. With Lill on Thunder leading the way, we headed north into the night.

We camped out in the open. I woke to a gentle gray dawn, thinking it had been one heck of a dream. I jumped to see Big Red above me, licking Rosey's face.

Lill laughed. She was already up, polishing Thunder's silver harness buckles with her sleeve.

Rosey listened, quiet, as we told her what happened. She didn't say anything, she just got up and walked Big Red out of sight. But it wasn't long before I could hear her bawling, apologizing through heaving tears to her horse for almost losing him.

"See what I mean?" Lill whispered to me. "You did good, trick roper."

Rosey came back, pretending we hadn't heard her, and we ate a bite -- cheese with some bread Lill had grabbed from the bar. We watched the morning sun rise up through the clouds, just the three of us camped out with our horses, nobody saying a thing. As if nothing at all had happened, as if the three of us living rough was the way it had always been.

TO FIND BUFFALO BILL

- 9 -

As much as Lill wanted Rosey to join us, she didn't gloat when it happened. There was never any big moment where Rosey announced she was coming with us to Cody. It was just sort of assumed.

We couldn't leave right away with Spackles still on the mend. So we went back to town to drum up some cash to see us on our way.

Lill's boss Pete wasn't such a bad fellow after all. He cooled down and felt bad about Rosey losing her house *and* her shop, and told Lill we could stay a while in the supply loft if we needed a place. That was fine with me, except that to get to the loft, we had to go through the saloon. That meant Rosey had to face the Hjodaddy boys. I was not looking forward to that.

The first time we went back to the saloon, all three of us, Lill and I flanked Rosey like a small pair of bookends holding an oversized volume. Two of the Hjodaddies were there. I never did learn to tell them apart.

"Well howdy there, Rosey," said one of them. "That's a mighty fine house you built."

She didn't reply.

"And an even finer work shed," said the other.

Again she didn't answer.

"We've been feeling bad about taking it from you," said the first. "So we decided to do something about it."

That got her attention. "You're going to give me my place back?" she asked.

"Better," said Hjodaddy number two. "We're going to let you

move in with us. We'll even let you cook, if you're very good."

Rosey stared at him. Lill and me bunched up close against her, as if we could stop her from taking them on. Then she folded her arms in front of her, like she was thinking it over, and she said, "I'll have to say no, Jim, on account of your fleas and everything. But it was a kind offer all the same."

The fellow shrugged, unoffended, since it was true. And just like that, Rosey wasn't upset anymore. She had lost her shop herself, she said, fair and square. It was a simple as that.

Then Pete asked Lill if she wanted her old job back, but she said no. She had other plans. And before the day was out, she was dragging us to every rancher around, and telling them how we'd branded Deek Runyan's mad steer. Folks scoffed at us at first, but word got around that we'd actually branded that troublesome steer. So we got jobs too dangerous for anyone else to do, catching the meanest animals you could imagine. It was good training, Lill said, for our cowgirling act. She chased the bulls down on black Thunder, I roped the thing, and Rosey would wrastle it to the ground. Rosey got paid to do it, and Lill told everybody in town to come watch. As I saw those ranch hands with their eyes as big as saucers, it made me proud.

We had just a couple of more jobs to finish up when a storm blew in from the north. With it came lightning, and brushfires, and much more nastiness than the floods of rain.

I remember the first time I saw Cilla, draped over the bar counter and talking to Pete. We ran in just as the storm hit and there she was, with a jaunty bandanna tried round her neck. She wore tooled leather boots and canvas pants, just like ours, but her cowgirling clothes looked staged. Like she was playing a part, not living a life. Something about her made me want to stay away.

Pete saw us and called us over. "Gals, this is Miss Priscilla Pystunia. Cilla, for short. We've been talking a spell, and she's got some information you might want to hear."

She looked us over, from Rosey's big arms, Lill's furry bear chaps, and my dried-out grass hat. Then she sniffed her nose in the air and said, "So one of you wants to ride for Buffalo Bill? Well, you can forget it. I just came from Cody, and he's not hiring."

"You mean..." said Rosey, "...that he's not hiring you? What are you supposed to be, anyway?"

"I'm a trick rider," said Cilla. The way she said it you would have thought she was the Duchess of France. "Did you see that horse outside? The gray one?"

I'd seen it, all right. Big and shaggy as if he hadn't been brushed all summer. Frankly, I'd half thought it was another Hjodaddy brother.

"He's a trick-riding horse," Priscilla said. "And he's all mine."

"Well, goody for you," said Rosey.

"Wait a minute," said Lill. "You said Bill ain't hiring. Did he tell you that himself?"

"He didn't have to," said Priscilla. "He's not even there. I guess he's off in Denver, or some such place. He's not even running a show."

Even Rosey didn't know what to say to that.

And Lill... well, Lill just flopped down onto a stool, her face kind of squashed up like the bottom of a pumpkin, and then she just let loose, bawling as loud as I'd ever seen.

Cilla's mouth dropped open as she watched Lill make a spectacle of herself.

I leaned over to explain to Cilla. "We were going to be cowgirls with Bill's show," I said. "It's been Lill's dream."

"All three of you?" said Cilla. "You were all going to join?"

I nodded. "Lill's a speed rider. I rope. And Rosey here, she can wrastle like you wouldn't believe."

Cilla looked at the three of us, one at a time. Then she said, "So what's the problem? We don't need Buffalo Bill. Or Pawnee Bill. Or any Bill at all. Heck, we don't need any man. There's four of us. We can make our own show."

Lill stopped spouting.

"That's right," said Cilla. "We got the talent. We've got the skills. All we have to do is put it together."

"You think so?" said Rosey. "You think we could make our own show, and do it so well that old Bill would be crazy not to star us?"

Lill sprung up from her stool, her crying fit completely forgotten. "Of course, we can. Ain't you seen how all those ranch fellows line up to see us go at it? You bet, they'll pay to see. They'll have to. Or else, they don't get to see what we do!"

"We'll need someone who can shoot," said Rosey. "All wild west shows have a shooter. And don't give me that look, Lill. You know that bear was a lucky shot."

"I'll shoot for you," said one of the Hjodaddies. "That's just what you little darlin's need is a good-looking fellow like me."

"No how!" said Lill. "We ain't taking no man. And especially not one of you grubs. It's all girls that ride with us. We're going to find us a lady shooter."

"I heard of a gal who was good with a rifle," said Pete. "Down in Big Piney."

"What are we waiting for?" said Lill.

Rosey chimed in. "Let's go find her."

"That's the spirit," said Cilla, slapping us on the back like she was already one of us.

That's how it was that those miserable, thieving Hjodaddy brothers, of all people, gave us our name -- the All-Girl No-Man Little Darlin's Wild West Show.

As we took off for Big Piney, I was glad. I was happy Lill had stopped her crying. I was pleased we had a plan. I was relieved Rosey hadn't gambled anything else away.

I was so glad for all these things that I didn't listen to that nagging little voice inside my head, that whispered I should be cautious. Because no matter how loud Cilla said all the right things, and made all the right sounds and motions, even at that magic moment when we formed our show, to me she never really felt like one of us.

THE BUCKET OF BLOOD

- 10 -

It was late afternoon when we got to Big Piney. We rode down the dusty main street, with houses and shops lined up on both sides. We found the saloon right away. It had a big red sign out front that said: *Welcome to the Bucket of Blood.*

We got off our horses and tied them to nearest post. Then Cilla, Lill, and Rosey walked up the wooden steps and headed in.

I wasn't ready to go inside just yet, with the sun about to set, casting the sky a pretty candy pink. Rosey questioned me with her eyes.

"You go ahead," I said to her. I'm taking a little stroll. I'll meet you later."

"I don't think we should split up," said Cilla. "How would you know where to find us?"

Lill and Rosey laughed. The whole town was so small you could walk every bit of it in ten minutes or less. Even a blind fool with one leg couldn't have got lost in a town that size.

"Good one," said Lill, patting Cilla on the shoulder like she'd just made a joke. But Cilla didn't think it was funny. Instead, she glared at me, annoyed I hadn't obeyed her idea.

I turned away and walked down to the end of the street. There was a plank walkway on the side and I took it, my steps so soft and quiet that they made no noise on the wooden slats.

I liked doing that.

The buildings in town were mostly tarred log cabins. I could see the logs joined up from the sides. Further down the street, the cabins had plank facades out front painted in soft pastel colors. It gave me a good feeling. As if the buildings weren't afraid to dream.

Near the end of the street, where North Piney Creek funneled in close to the road, I saw a woman carrying a basket of laundry. As she walked past, and I looked down at her basket. Force of habit, I guess, to see if something needed some sewing.

She stopped and appraised me. "Does my wash interest you, stranger?" she said, in a chipped German accent.

"Maybe," I said. "If it needs mending and somebody wants to pay for it. Although I didn't come here for that. My friends and I are looking for someone. We heard there was a lady shooter that lived down this way. Do you know who I mean?"

She shrugged. "I think perhaps you have wasted your time."

"That wouldn't be a first."

I walked further down until I got to the very last little shack. I stood there at the end of the town, watching the clouds go from pink to purple. When they started to turn lavender blue, I headed back up the street.

As I was half-way to the saloon, a lady came out of a building.

"I want to talk to you," she said.

Who would be talking to me? I knew nobody in this town. I kept going.

"Stop," she said. "I know who you are."

I turned to face her, confused.

She stood beside a two story building labeled "Cafe and Bakery." Her sleeves were rolled up and her hands were dusted with flour. But what I noticed most was that she wore a skirt. Not an ankle skirt, what most ladies of the time wore, but an older style that went all the way to the ground.

Just like the kind my Mama wore.

I froze up inside.

She marched up to me, wiping flour off her hands.

I couldn't move, shivering with thoughts of search parties sent by my mother to drag me back east.

My head went dizzy, my stomach fell sick.

"Klara says you're looking for a shooter," said the woman in the long skirt. "Well, here I am."

It took me a moment to realize she hadn't meant to shoot me.

She frowned. "Did you want to see me or not?"

"You don't look like any shooter I ever saw."

She said, "I probably don't look like the best cook you'll ever see, either. But I might be. What did you want?"

I didn't know what to say. I was good with rope, not with words. "Come meet Lill and Rosey," I told her. "They'll say it better than me."

*

We sat just outside the saloon on the plank sidewalk. Cilla pouted the whole time, as if annoyed it was me that found the sharp shooter. I was already learning to ignore her moods.

Klara, the woman with the laundry basket, joined us, standing quietly behind the shooter gal in the long skirt.

Lill explained who we were, and what we had in mind. The long-skirt woman, Violet, told us her story. She had come from New York, lured by love letters from a sweet-talking man she'd never met who lived way out in Casper, Wyoming. So sure of her man, she convinced Klara to come along with her, assured that her sweetheart had a bachelor brother who was too handsome for words.

So Violet and Klara came west. Violet had come from a family of seven sisters who were glad to have one less mouth to feed. And Klara had come over from Germany with her mother, who caught fever and died just before they landed at Ellis Island.

Between them, Violet and Klara scraped together everything they could to get a one-way train ticket to Casper. But when they got there, they found out they'd been had. Violet's "fellow" had no brother or honorable intent. Instead, he ran a house of ill-repute. When they arrived, he had their bags whisked away to his place and then told them the facts. He said they had no choice but to work for him now, with no place to go and nowhere to turn. He insisted they had no choice but to work for him, since they'd never make it on their own.

They went to his place with him, but had no intention of staying. That first night, just as soon as that man turned his back, they managed to escape. But somehow in the scuffle, they lost their suitcases, and escaped with nothing more than the clothes on their backs and the love letters Violet kept in her corset close to her heart.

Like a pair of tumbleweeds, they blew around until the wind dropped them there in Big Piney, with Violet cooking for the cafe and Klara doing the wash.

With her first money, Violet bought a gun and blasted holes in those love letters from that evil man. According to Klara, Vi was good at that, shooting the most hurtful lies right out of the paper until there was nothing left of those letters but her rage.

But Klara didn't buy a gun. Instead, Klara bought a cow.

Lill was desperate to get Violet for the show. But Violet wasn't so sure. In the end, it wasn't us that convinced her – it was Klara.

"This town is too small," said Klara. "I want to be in their show."

"You?" Cilla asked Klara. "What can you do for the Little Darlin's?"

"I can ride a cow," said Klara, as if it was the most obvious thing in the world.

We stared at each other for a moment. Trust Cilla to be blunter than a chipped spoon.

"We don't need a clown," Cilla said. "I'm not putting on that kind of show. I refuse. I just won't do it."

"Klara's not a clown," said Violet. "And you should know that it's not easy to ride a cow. Have you ever tried it? They're jittery and bony and stubborn. Much worse than a horse. And I don't even ride those, if I can help it."

"You don't ride?" said Cilla. "I thought you said you had a horse."

"I do, but I don't like to ride unless I have to. I'm not very comfortable up there."

"What kind of useless cowgirl are you?" said Cilla.

"Annie Oakley couldn't ride either," I said, "before she signed up with Buffalo Bill."

"But she learned," said Cilla.

"And so will Vi," said Lill. "At least good enough to be in the show."

"I haven't agreed," Vi told us. "And I won't even consider it, unless you take Klara, too."

"Enough talking," said Lill. "This isn't getting us anywhere. Let's do a practice. We'll show you what we do and you show us yours. After that, we can haggle it out."

It was so sensible that even Cilla couldn't disagree.

PINEY CREEK SHOW

- 11 -

This show-off was to convince Vi, the lady shooter, that we were worth her time. It was also a test, to see if she was worth ours, along with Klara on her cow. But it was more than that. Lill wanted to see if we could pull a real crowd who would pay, not just the gawkers we had before. Something worth watching. Something worth being part of.

It was Lill and Cilla who planned it all out. They decided who would stand where, and what order we'd go in. They wrote it all down, a tidy little program with the two of them taking turns announcing each act.

While they put the schedule together, Vi and Klara went to find us a pasture. Cilla had wanted to use Klara's cow for the roping, but Klara wouldn't have it. It was hard enough on her cow to be ridden, she said, let alone be roped and wrastled to the ground. So Klara and Vi had to scrounge up a steer, too, one that was wild enough to make us look good.

I wove myself a couple of ropes, and made some tack for Klara. She wanted a special muzzle for her cow, and also for her horse, Lady, a small buckskin mare with a nasty habit of biting when you didn't expect it. Both rope harnesses were easy to make, especially for the cow since it had no hardware or bit. Instead, it was just a face collar with a loop on the back to hang onto. Klara said that was all she needed. I made just what she asked for, though I couldn't imagine how she could steer anything with that.

Rosey hammered a sheet of tin into a megaphone. I lined up her tools and watched as she bent the metal until it was just the right shape. I never got tired of watching her work, the way her hands spoke to the metal. It was different than working thread or rope -- a rougher language, but eloquent in its own way.

Vi and Klara secured a pasture with a wild bull to boot. By the time they came back to tell us, the megaphone was done, my ropes were done, and the show was all planned out. We had everything ready. Everything but the crowd.

We didn't all agree on that. Vi didn't want on-lookers. But Lil insisted it was part of the test -- for all of us.

"Are you scared your aim's not up to it?" Cilla goaded Vi.

"She shoots very well," said Klara.

"Then prove it," said Cilla. "In front of all of us. And anyone else who wants to watch."

Vi still didn't like the idea. So we did the only thing that was fair. We took a vote.

I was curious to see if we could draw a crowd. But I didn't like how pushy Cilla was being, so I sided with Vi. Or maybe I was just voting against Cilla. Klara, not wanting to hurt her chances to get in, chose not to vote. So with Rosey and Cilla siding with Lill, she won.

I was afraid that Vi would walk out right then, but she didn't. She stuck to her word and agreed to Lill's show.

It was Lill and Cilla who went all over town, talking up the event. Oh my, could those girls talk! You would have thought we'd be turning grass into gold instead of performing a handful of cowgirling stunts. And later that day, before the sun went down, we crossed Big Piney Creek to do our first show.

We rode into the field in single file, like a parade with Cilla in front on her gray horse, and Lill right behind her on Thunder, as proud as could be.

Behind them was Klara riding Lady, her nippy little buckskin horse, now muzzled with the nose wrap I made her. Roped to them was Klara's fat cow, Sugar, who toddled alongside, her droopy pink udder slapping her thighs with every step.

Then came was Vi, still wearing her big skirt, perched uncomfortably on her brown mare, who was named Prize. It was the first time I'd seen Violet's horse, and now I knew why she kept it hidden away. Prize was the oldest, ugliest horse I'd ever seen -- mud brown with a back that swayed to nearly her hocks. I rode behind Violet, with a perfect hind view of Prize's tail, which had been half chewed-off by some goat. After the goat chewed it, as if in sympathy, most of the Prize's mane had fallen off, too.

It was painful to watch Violet riding that plodding old bald horse, with Vi's knees shaking as her skirt billowed up, and her legs sticking out like pieces of wood.

I knew Vi had said she didn't like to ride, but I had never seen a rider less comfortable in the saddle. It did not bode well for her cowgirling skills.

Spackles walked slow, keeping a healthy distance between old Prize and us, as if old age was catching. And Rosey, on Big Red, brought up the rear.

"They're coming," Rosey called from behind me. I looked around me to see what she meant. There, following behind us, was what looked like the entire town coming along to be entertained.

"So many people!" said Rosey. "Maybe we should have practiced more first."

"You voted for this," I said. "You get what you asked for."

I felt nervous to have such a crowd watch us. Part of me agreed with Cilla, that Klara's cow riding sounded like a ripe old embarrassment. Though I'd never tell Cilla I agreed with her.

Even more worrisome, we hadn't seen Violet shoot. What if she couldn't? It was only Klara's word that Violet was a sure shot, and Klara wanted out of this town because she was tired of doing its wash.

That's when I realized what else looked wrong.

I hadn't seen Vi with a gun. And as we rode into the field, I couldn't see one on her now, either.

But it was too late to stop the impending drama of our very first, and maybe our very last show.

The six of us Darlin's rode into the field while the townspeople made a large circle around us. Cilla and Lill stayed near the crowd. Vi and I rode along the border to the left, while Klara and Rosey rode off to the right. We stretched ourselves out in a half-circle defining "the ring."

Cilla got off her gray horse and faced the crowd. "Ladies and Gentleman," she called out through the megaphone, her voice loud and tinny. "Preeee-senting Lilly Geller on Black Thunder, the fastest horse in all the west!"

Lill blasted into the arena, leaning into that horse so deep that she looked like an arrow shot out of a bow.

She rode to the far end of the circle, and then beyond it. When she was just a black smudge in the distance, she came thundering back, heading straight for Cilla and the crowd. She was going so fast I didn't think she could stop in time as she ploughed straight for the crowd. The people screamed and fled like scared chickens about to be tromped. I thought I might have to save them; my rope itched in my hands, though no way could I save them all.

Then like magic, Thunder came to a dead stop right before the gasping crowd. The people, once they got over the shock, applauded with zest. Lill beamed as Thunder preened, showing off his glossy form.

Lill jumped off Thunder and bowed to the crowd, throwing kisses to her adoring fans while Thunder pranced and posed beside her.

For me, that's the moment our show became real. I didn't even care anymore if Vi could shoot or not. At that second, Klara could ride a duck for all I cared. If nothing else went right that day, the whole thing was worth it to see Lilly up there taking her bows, her joy pouring out, as if the sun shone extra bright on her that day. It warmed me to my toes, to see that her dream, the one she had shaped with her will, was every bit as good as she hoped it would be.

But I also saw Cilla grimace, the sour taint of envy full on her face.

Once the crowd's cheering quieted down, Lill took the megaphone to announce the next act. And while Lill was not large, her voice was a powerhouse. I don't know if she needed that tin contraption to be heard, the way her excitement just boomed out of her.

"Hello, Big Piney!" she called. "Yes, sir. That was Black Thunder. What a horse! He's really something, isn't he? But that's not all. Because for our next amazing feat, here comes your very own, home-grown, Miss Violet Eubanks, sharp shooter extrordinare as she performs feats of marksmanship that will amaze and astound you. Assisting her is another local star, Klara Vogel."

Violet, finally off old Prize, took a deep breath and walked to the center of the ring. Klara left her horse and cow and joined Violet, with a small item in her hands. Everyone strained their eyes to see what it was, far too small to be a gun.

They said something in private, then Vi took 30 steps towards the crowd, pacing it off in careful measures.

When she stopped, I could see what Klara was holding. It was a candle. She lit a match to it, then held it above her head like the Statue of Liberty.

At that point, Vi reached under her big skirt and pulled out one of the longest rifles I'd ever seen. I don't know how she fit it under her skirt, but there it was, cocked and ready. She aimed it at Klara's head, or maybe just a notch above, while Klara stood there, as calm as a pond on a wind-free day.

But I was shaking in my boots. I knew Klara was supposed to help with the target, but not one of us knew -- not even Lill, that Klara was the target.

I covered my ears and shut my eyes, too. I didn't know Klara that well, but I didn't want to see her in pieces.

Out rang a shot.

I peeked through my fingers.

Amazingly enough, Klara was still there.

Only the candle flame was gone -- nearly shot out!

The people went wild with applause, and me, too. Klara smiled smugly. I didn't need to know German to know the *I-told-you-so* look on her face.

As for Vi, her cheeks flushed pink, but she didn't look exactly pleased. She seemed embarrassed by what she'd done, by what she could do.

I heard one voice in the crowd above the rest. It called out: "That was a lucky shot. I'll bet she can't do it again!"

I craned my neck around to see who had said it. It was to the left of the crowd, with nobody from the audience there. All I could see was one person half-hidden, crouched behind a small tree.

Cilla?

"Yeah," shouted someone else. "Do it again!"

Vi gave a reluctant nod and reloaded her gun. Klara lit the candle with another match and held it back up. This time I didn't cover my eyes as Vi sighted it in, squeezed off her shot, and blasted the flame out.

The people clapped.

"Again!" someone called. Not Cilla this time.

Klara re-lit the candle, and held it up. Vi gave a reluctant sigh, but went ahead and re-loaded her gun. Then she targeted it in, taking her time to site it in since the candle was shorter now, with its flame much closer to Klara's head. And once again, she shot the candle's fire out.

I looked over at the tree where Cilla was hiding. Surely she wouldn't dare say anything more.

"One more time!" came her voice, taunting.

The crowd took up her chant, demanding more. "One more time!" they shouted.

Klara looked at the candle, not more than a nub by this point. I could see she wasn't happy about this. Vi wasn't either. But she said something to Klara I couldn't hear, and Klara lit the candle stub one more time.

This time, Klara counted to three and threw the candle straight up. Violet shot it in the air, blasting it to a waxy nothing.

The people cheered and whistled as Vi and Klara walked back to the fence. I realized that none of these people, except for Klara, had seen Violet shoot before. She could do this remarkable skill, but rarely let it out from her skirt.

In that moment, I understood something about Vi. She didn't want fame or attention. I could see she what she wanted out of life. It was exactly what my mother had wanted for me -- to be a lady of taste and refinement. But along the way Vi had taken a wrong turn, and now had to reply on an unladylike skill.

"Wasn't that just dandy?" Lill called out to the crowd. "And now, Klara's going to do a trick of her own. Introducing the amazing Klara Vogel. And her fabulous cow Sugar, who you've seen plenty of times. But never like this."

As Klara led Sugar into the ring, the cow seemed oblivious to everything but chewing her cud. That cow was so placid it might as well have been a chair. I just couldn't see how this was going to entertaining at all.

Somehow, after Violet's shooting, Klara had donned a long scarf and a leather helmet, like what an aviatrix would wear.

She looked absurd as she led Sugar to the center of the ring.

There she stopped and held the scarf out to its full length, facing north, then the east, and then south and west, gauging the wind.

When she was satisfied, she tugged the cow into a particular direction, then leapt onto Sugar's back.

Sugar's eyes went white with excitement. She took off like a cannon, racing with more speed than I'd seen any cow muster. With one hand, Klara hung on to the loop, spanking her gently with a crop to switch her this way and that. Sugar's gait was choppy, bouncing Klara up and down like a bobbin. I don't know how but Klara didn't fall off -- she rode like she was part of that cow. I could hardly believe my eyes when they reached the edge of the field where Klara lept off, like an acrobat.

Sugar trotted to a stop. Klara led her away and that cow just waddled along, no longer a speed racer, just a big fat bovine chewing her cud. It was one heck of an act, far more exciting than I ever expected from watching a cow.

But I didn't have time to clap. It was time for me to come out. Cilla, now back in the ring, had the megaphone to announce me. I don't remember what she said or how the crowd looked. When it was my turn, everything else blurred and melted away except for my focus. That's how it was for me. When those moments took hold, there weren't nothing in the whole world but me and my rope and that target.

I stood where we'd planned it and readied my rope. But something wasn't right. I looked around and saw Rosey, clearly annoyed. I followed her gaze to see what was wrong.

And then I saw it, too. Or rather, I didn't see it.

The rancher had told us his mean bull kept to itself, and that he'd have no trouble chasing it in. But there was no lone bull in that field. Instead, what came towards me was a whole herd of cattle with several bulls mixed in. I didn't know where to aim or which bull I was meant to rope.

Lill rode Thunder out to the herd of cattle. There was no way she could tell which bull we were supposed to catch, either.

But Thunder knew. That horse was a natural born cutter. He

sniffed the one bull who didn't smell like the rest, and zipped in behind him, forcing him away from the pack until he had that big nasty bull running exactly where he was supposed to go -- straight towards me.

I stood my ground, my rope ready, watching that bull come into my range. He was a hefty one, all right, and mad crazy with rage. I reached out to throw, but something inside me told me to hold fast. In another few heartbeats I saw why. That bull wasn't coming straight, the crafty old thing was zig-zagging towards me, dodging and weaving as he ran. Had I thrown my rope that first time, I surely would have missed.

There was nothing I could do but wait until I was sure he was done dodging. I held my breath until he made his final run at me, horns down, charging in for the kill.

Rosie called out something to me; I can't recall what she said. I needed all my attention to gauge my shot. I would only get one chance and it had to be right.

He came at me, snorting and heaving, closing in with every second. My rope had to catch. It just had to.

My heart slowed, my hand did not shake. I watched the knot fly away from me and arc up into the sky. The bull was so close I could see red in his eye and smell his musk. I knew he would have me in another second or two if the loop missed.

All time stood still. There wasn't nothing I could do now -- whatever happened, my fate was already sealed.

The loop of the rope wobbled and danced in the air as if it was a living thing acting all on its own.

Then it came down, reaching out for the bull. And landed square on its sweaty neck.

But still that bull came.

Then something banged into me. It was Rosey, pushing me aside as she took the rope end from me. She ran it out to the right, yanking it tight.

That's when I remembered my second rope, coiled around my other arm. I twirled it up and landed that one on the bull's neck, too. Then I ran it left. Now we had him tied from both sides. There was nowhere for him to go but down. Which was Rosie's job.

She approached from the side, then reached for his horns and jerked his head to the side. But instead of pulling away like she expected, he plowed his head down. This threw Rosey over his head. She looked like a rag doll flopping in the air, and landed with a thud in the dirt in front of him, as angry as I'd ever seen her. She picked herself up, dusted off her pants, and came at him from the other side.

When she yanked his horns, this time as he snapped his head under, she was ready. She jerked his head down even more. As his head hit the dirt, his own momentum flipped the rest of him over. He landed back down, feet up. Just right for trussing up. Rosey got in there quick and tied him up like a present, with his legs wrapped tight together with a tidy bow.

I thought she'd be mad at me, for waiting so long for my first toss, and getting so hypnotized by that bull's power that I nearly forgot my second.

But not Rosey. "I wish all bulls were this dumb," she said as she flashed me a big grin. "Can you imagine, trying to pull the same head-down trick on me twice?"

"Are you okay?" I asked. I knew the flip had landed her hard on her back.

"Sure," she told me. But I noticed as we walked out that she had a slight limp.

That's when I remembered the crowd. I heard them cheer. They were proud of us. Proud of Lill and Rosey and all of us Darlin's.

And proud of me. A whole wall of people, clapping for me. As if I was special. As if I mattered. I'd only felt that way once before, when I had that summer with Papa. It was like he was there with me, all over again. I was so happy I thought I'd split wide open.

"Wait!" Cilla shouted into her megaphone. "There's more. After that display, you want to see more incredible rope tricks, don't you?"

"More, more!" called the crowd.

"And more you'll have," said Cilla. "Because our trick roper, Maisy, is going to perform a stunt called 'spinning the wedding ring'. Come on, Maisy. Show us your stuff."

Rosey stopped walking and stared at me, confused, then a little hurt. As if I had some wonderful new trick up my sleeve and hadn't even told her about it.

"She's making things up," I told Rosey. "I don't know that trick." I shrugged to the crowd.

"My mistake," said Cilla. "Maisy's trick isn't the wedding ring. She's going to do... the ocean wave!"

I shook my head again. Megaphone or not, Cilla wasn't about to tell me what to do. "She's lying," I told Rosey. "I don't know what she's talking about. Let's get out of here. I'm done."

As we walked out, the crowd no longer cheered for me. They went silent, like they felt cheated that I was holding back some fancy trick.

Thank goodness for Lill. She seized the megaphone from Cilla. "Wasn't that catch just dandy?" she said. "That bull has been giving the Owens crew the slip for some time now. But this time, it's the old bull that got slipped. Wasn't that great folks? So lets hear it again for Maisy and Rosey, the best roper-wrastler team you'll ever see."

The people did applaud. But not as loud as before.

Rosey noticed it, too. "At least now that we're done," she said with a shrug, "we can enjoy the rest of the show."

But the show was nearly done. All that was left was Cilla and her trick riding. Lill put this in last as our big bang show-stopper ending.

Rosey and I met up with Vi and Klara at the edge of the ring. We'd never actually seen Cilla's act on her fancy registered trick horse. We hadn't even seen her rehearse. We watched with the crowd, ready to be impressed.

Cilla rode into the ring on her big gray gelding. The horse didn't look as shaggy as before. I guess Lill showed her how to brush him out. But even with grooming, the gray horse was never going to be as sleek and glossy as black Thunder.

"Announcing Miss Priscilla Pystunia," said Lill, "our trick rider and final star feature, will now perform for you... the *flag hand.*"

Cilla rode into the ring waving one hand in the air. I watched her go, waiting for the trick. She rode from one side of the ring to the other, waving her hand. When she got to the edge, she got off her horse. And bowed.

"Did I miss it?" said Vi. "Where was the trick? Klara, did you see it?"

Klara shook her head. We looked at each other, every one of us confused.

Then from inside me, a fit of giggles escaped. I couldn't help it.

"Where was the trick?" Rosie asked.

"Don't you see?" I told her. " 'Flag hand.' She rode with one hand. That WAS the 'trick!' "

Rosey, Klara and Vi stared at me like I was a fool to suggest such a thing. "Don't blame me," I said. "It's HER idea of a trick, not mine."

From the ring Lill called out. "And now, ladies and gentlemen. Miss Priscilla will perform... the double flag hand!"

Cilla pointed her horse towards the right side of the ring. Then she wrapped the reins around the horn of her saddle, her face anxious with fear. The horse, as if sensing her nervousness, picked his way ever so gently to the far side of the ring, as carefully as if he was carrying a basket of eggs. This time, Cilla waved *both* her hands in the air.

"See?" I said to Rosey, Klara, and Violet. "You get it now? The *double* flag?"

Rosey snickered. But Violet looked horrified. Then she started to clap her hands for all she was worth. "Quick," she said. "Act impressed. This is our fellow cowgirl out there. We can't let her down."

Klara shrugged. "I can clap," she said, "for the horse." Then she shouted, "Bravo! Bravo!" to try to help Violet whip up the crowd.

Rosey and I looked at each other, then we added our noise, too. We had a lot of it, since it was the only way to hide how hard we were laughing, to think of Cilla concentrating so hard with her silly hands flopping around in the air.

The crowd was confused. But then something funny happened. An old man clapped, then a boy. It caught on until everybody was clapping. They weren't sure what they'd missed but they didn't want to be left out. Cilla climbed down from her saddle, pleased as punch to have made such a stir. It made me think of a story I'd heard in school, before Mama wouldn't let me go anymore, about an Emperor from far away and his invisible new clothes that everyone pretended they'd seen.

Lill waved us all to the center of the ring and we joined her there to wrap up the show. We faced the crowd, all six of us Darlin's, holding hands, with Cilla on the far end next to Lill, because none of the rest of us could look our trick rider in the eye just yet.

With Cilla on the opposite end, I could forget about her as I looked out at all those people cheering and whistling at all they had seen. Right then, the world seemed mighty fine. I was fine. I was a cowgirl, a true blue hero of the wild west. For the second time in my life, I felt I was exactly who I was supposed to be.

VIOLET AND KLARA DECIDE

- 12 -

Mr. Owens, the fellow whose bull we chased down, was so pleased about getting his bull roped up that he said we could stay in his back cabin as long as we wanted. It was an empty lookout post on the far end of his ranch that he used from time to time to watch out for rustlers. It hadn't been cleaned in a while so Lill and Cilla went to tidy it up while Klara and Violet went back to town to pack up their things. Rosey and I rode back to our campsite. It didn't take us long to get the wagon and load up our gear and Rosey's tools. That was the good thing about the travelling life. We didn't have much, so we didn't have much to worry about.

I sat up front in the wagon with Rosey while Spackles and Big Red pulled it. But Big Red drooped his head and Spackles balked, stopping at what felt like every single weed along the way. Spackles was cranky even with other horses. So we unhooked her and tied her up to the back, and had Big Red pull it himself. He liked that. We could see his ears perk up.

"I would have thought Big Red would have liked the help," I said to Rosey.

She shook her head. "I think he felt insulted. Like we didn't trust him to pull it himself."

I thought about that as I watched Big Red trot along now with a bounce in his gait. He seemed pleased to be out front, strong and powerful, without needing to match his pace with anybody else. I never thought about it that way before, that a cart horse could be proud of his job. Spackles didn't like work at all. To be honest, she didn't like much of anything except her food, and even when she was eating, she rolled her eyes as if it was never quite tasty enough.

"There it is," said Rosey, nodding towards a mossy cabin in the distance. It stood by itself against the backdrop of the Tetons. After sleeping under the stars, it looked like a palace.

When we got there, we found our "palace" was a 10 x 12' box. Everything was small, even the door. I could tell we'd all have to duck to go through it, except maybe Lill. It was going to be a tight fit for six of us crammed into those wall-to-wall bunks.

Lill, sweeping the floor, scolded us. "For Heaven's sake," she said, "take off your boots." Already I was starting to regret cabin life, because it came with rules.

Cilla was inside, too, on a lower bunk, the widest, that she'd claimed for herself. She was arranging the curtain on the room's only window. The curtain was made from a burlap bag with red letters stamped on the side. The smell was faint, but I could tell what that bag once held -- fifty pounds of sweet feed. A big part of me wished the label on the side said the sack had come from my Papa's feed store.

Cilla saw me looking at her window. "I've been thinking," she said. "Lill says you sew. Can you make us a banner? A big sign that says *The Little Darlin's* stretched out across the front?"

I nodded. Gosh, anyone could have done that.

Rosey said, "Wasn't that something, the way Violet shot? Old Pete didn't steer us wrong when he told us about her. I'll bet she's better than Annie Oakley herself."

"Oakley's half blind," said Cilla. "Anyone can shoot better than a blind woman. Besides, Violet was supposed to shoot the candle out. But that last time, she missed. Because when the pieces landed, I could see the part with the wick was still lit."

My mouth dropped open. Who was *Miss Flag Hands* to complain about Violet's aim?

I was about to say something when the rickety door opened and Vi and Klara walked in. Klara held two satchels, one in each hand, while Vi carried a towel wrapped around something warm. She'd brought us food -- a hot home-cooked meal, delivered and everything.

And what did she get in return? To walk in on Cilla's disrespect.

I was so ashamed of Cilla I could barely look at her. I hoped Violet hadn't heard. If she did, she didn't let on.

"This is pie," said Klara. "Pork and apple."

Vi peeled the towel away revealing two separate pie mounds of perfect crust. The aroma steamed out into every square inch of that cabin.

Lill laughed. "I didn't even know I was hungry, but now I can't wait. Which pie is which?"

"They're both the same," said Klara. "The meat and apple is mixed.

"Don't worry," Violet said. "It's better than it sounds."

I didn't know how that could be true, because it already sounded delicious.

I got our tin plates from the wagon and Violet divided the pies. The only place to sit was on the bunks, so we each claimed our territory. There were just four bunks, so Violet and Klara agreed to share the other bottom bunk. I took the top shelf above them. Rosey, too long for any of the beds, made herself at home on the floor.

As we sat in our spots, Vi passed out the wedges of pie. Lill had a bucket of clean water she hadn't used for scrubbing yet, and we passed that around, taking sips from the dipper.

I wondered what Mama would have thought, to see me eating with my hand, washing it down with water from a scrub pail. But I swear, I never had a better meal. We must have all felt that way because none of us said a thing, not even Lill, as we savored the tender meat and tangy apple nestled in that buttery crust.

In no time at all, both pies were picked clean. I was almost too stuffed to think.

Lill smiled at Klara and Violet. "Did you both make them?"

Klara shook her head. "Violet is the cook," she said. "I only clean. Although sometimes I pound the dough. It's much like squeezing the laundry."

She hadn't meant it as a joke but we all laughed. Klara had a way of saying things I didn't expect.

Rosey, on her spot on the floor, seemed to agree. "You and that cow," she said. "I couldn't believe when it ran like that. I don't know how you stayed on."

"That was some cow riding, all right," said Lill. "Who would have thought?"

"Why were you checking the wind?" I asked Klara.

Lill said, "Was that for the build-up? To bump up the tension for your act?"

Klara shook her head. "Sugar doesn't like the wind to blow up her tail. Her udder gets cold. When that happens, she goes very fast. Silly cow, to think she can run from the wind. The wind tells me which way she will run. This tells me how hard to hang on."

"I used to make rivets for boats," said Rosey. "It sounds to me like what you're saying is that Sugar's milk bag is like a big old rudder, and you catch the wind on it and sail her like a ship in the breeze."

Klara thought about that.

Lill started to laugh. "So what you're saying is, Klara flies the cow like a kite."

We all laughed, too, not just because it was such a silly notion but because in a way, it was true.

Only Violet didn't laugh. She hadn't said much at all. I wasn't the only one who noticed how quiet she'd been.

"Enough joking around," said Cilla. "We've got some serious things to decide. For one thing, are you both wanting to join? I see two satchels, but so far, Violet, you haven't agreed to our terms. We won't accept Klara with us until you agree to perform in every one of our shows, wherever we go, until I say so."

"You?" I said. "Who made you the queen of us?"

Lill cut in. "Cilla has a point. We need a sharp shooter. Violet needs to agree to our terms."

Klara looked nervous. It was clear she wanted to come with us. She didn't seem sure what Violet would say.

If Violet was chaffed by Cilla's rudeness, she didn't let on. "To be honest," she said, "I don't like shooting like that. With all those people watching."

"It didn't hurt your aim," said Rosey.

"That's not the problem," said Vi. "I always hit what I shoot, no matter what. I didn't work hard for this, it just comes to me. But it's not something I'm proud of, or want to be known for. If it gets me and Klara out of Big Piney, fine. But I don't want to do it all my life."

"Wait a minute," I said. "You shoot like that but you don't even practice?"

Violet shook her head. "I guess what I'm trying to say is that it feels like... like I'm showing off."

"Of course you're showing off!" said Lill. "That's the whole point."

"It's not *my* point," said Vi. "That's not what I want."

Lill couldn't believe it. Her dream was so real in her head, she couldn't imagine anyone else not wanting it.

I didn't understand it either. Doing that show, we were part of a team. It was the best thing that ever happened to me. I couldn't imagine anything to top it.

"What *do* you want?" Rosey asked.

"I want what every girl wants," said Vi. "I want true love. My own man, one who'll be mine forever and ever, like you read about in *Ranch Romance*. I don't think shooting will get me that. You can't blast your way into a man's heart. Or get there by doing tricks."

Lill frowned. "You want to bake your way in?"

Violet nodded. "Isn't that what you all want? To be Mrs. Somebody? Deep down, isn't that what every one of you wants?"

We were all quiet. I couldn't tell what people were thinking. I looked at Violet, sitting there in her old-fashioned skirt, saying out loud exactly what Mama always wanted for me. I didn't want that for myself. But would I change my mind? Could it be true that Mama was right after all?

Then Rosey sat up. And I thought, please, not Rosey, too. Because if Rosey the wrastler agreed with Violet, I didn't know how I could hold out.

"A man?" Rosey said. "You think every gal wants a man? Shoot, when the Hjodaddy brothers asked me to move in with them, I could have had the pick of the litter, and my shop back, too. Hell, I could have had all five at once, if I wanted. Like a queen bee, with all my little dudes doing my bidding. And don't think I didn't consider it. *For one second.* But that was enough time to waste on such nonsense, because it would have bored me senseless. You think every gal is pining away to find herself a man? Not this Darlin'. Not this one at all."

I knew right then and there that whatever happened down the road, for that speech alone, I'd be grateful to Rosey for the rest of my life.

"You want to stay here?" Lill asked Violet, "while we take Klara with us?"

Vi shook her head. "There's no one here for me. I've kicked around this town long enough to know that. My true love's not here. He's out there, somewhere. So I'll come with you. I'll join your group. I will do your shows. But only until I find him. Then I'll leave you for him. I want you to know that's how it has to be. If you still want me, that is."

The room went silent a moment.

Then Cilla said, "This is important. We'll have to vote."

"Vote?" said Lill. "What's to consider? We got here a woman who knows her own mind, and her heart, too. There's nothing wrong with that. Besides, she shoots like a dream. If there's anyone who don't want Vi, you say so right now. You speak up loud, too, so we can vote you into the floor."

Cilla wanted to complain, but she shut her mouth.

Lill looked around. "Is that it? No nay-sayers? Good. Klara, Violet, it's official. You're both Little Darlin's now. And the first rule of being a Darlin' is this: we're here because we want to be. If anyone wants out, if anyone wants to quit the cowgirling life and walk away, for any reason at all, it's only a doorknob away. Will that suit you, Violet?"

For the first time that night, Violet smiled. "Yes, Lilly. Thank you. Thank you, all. It suits me just fine."

MAISY SMELLS A RAT

- 13 -

I woke up in my top bunk, the ceiling joist not far from my face. Usually when I woke up in a new place, my first thought was panic as I struggled to remember how I got there.

But not that morning. I knew exactly where I was.

The night had been cool, so I'd wrapped myself good before wedging into the crawl space between my bunk and the ceiling.

Lill's top bunk was empty. She was often the first one up.

Cilla, in the bunk below hers, was rolled up in a ball, snoring like sandpaper on bark. Rosey wasn't up either, stretched out on the floor.

But something had woke me up. It was a smell. A real good one.

Violet was making pancakes and pine syrup. I couldn't believe how she could turn wormy flour, some butter and sugar, and the trees outside into something that smelled so darn delicious. Selfishly, I hoped it would take her a very long time to find Mr. True Love.

I squeezed out my bunk and shimmied down, making plenty of noise. Rosey's head popped out from her blanket. "I dreamed of flap jacks," she said. "And here they are, right in front of me."

Violet smiled as if it was nothing it all. Maybe it wasn't, with a full-stocked kitchen and all the right pans. But to make them like that, thick and soft on top of a wood stove, that was talent, all right.

I got the plates we cleaned from last night. Lill came in from outside and we passed them around, each plate stacked with three pancakes, topped with butter and sweet sticky pine juice.

"Nothing to it," said Violet. "You fry up your batter and the syrup simmers itself. I just scoot it along."

Violet wasn't being fake modest. It really was dead easy for her.

By now we were all awake but Klara, huddled under her blanket.

"Rise and shine," Lill said, about to yank Klara's covers off.

"Let her sleep," said Vi. "She was up all hours finishing the whole week's washing. She wouldn't leave until she'd finished all her chores. Besides, Klara's a demon if you wake her up before she's ready."

I could see Klara working overtime to finish her jobs. It was harder to picture her snappy.

"Too bad," said Lill. "I have a secret surprise to show everyone. I have it right here in my hands. I guess it'll have to wait."

"What you got?" Rosey asked. "You know waiting is not one of your skills."

Lill shrugged. "Since you forced it out of me..." Then she held out her hat, brim up, and jingled it. It was lined with coins!

"Let me see," said Rosey, snatching the hat from Lill's hand. Lill smiled from ear to ear as Rosey beheld the treasure.

"Jumping gophers," said Rosey, "Where'd all this come from?"

"From the show," said Lill. "When the people were clapping and carrying on, I passed my hat around. I didn't ask or nothing. And look what they did!"

I could hardly believe it. There must have been half an inch of coins in the hat. I had never seen so much money in one place.

"Mostly everyone put something in," Lill told us. "All without asking."

We all marveled at that. Was it for the show? Or a fond send-off for Klara and Violet? Either way, it made me feel a special warmth for the folks of Big Piney.

Cilla sniffed up her nose. "No bills," she said. "Just change. We can do better. Which reminds me, Maisy. About your act yesterday..."

I was glad she brought it up. It needed discussing, that she didn't have the right to call out tricks I didn't know. It was about time she apologized for her behavior.

Then she added, "You should have done that trick when I asked for it."

"Me?" I said. "I did my trick. With serious danger."

She huffed. "You need to learn the *Wedding Ring* and *Ocean Wave*, to call yourself a real roper."

"Maybe you should learn a real trick," I said. "Before you embarrass us all again. Flag hands? That was no trick, that was baby riding."

"It's in the OFFICIAL book of trick riding," she said. "How would you know? Obviously, you never read it."

"How dare you try to make me look bad. In front of all those people. But it didn't work, did it? You're the one to be sorry."

It was so obvious to me what Cilla was up to. I expected everyone to back me up.

Violet faded back to the wall. I was to learn she didn't like confrontation, of any kind.

Lill stayed where she was, her concern etched in her face. Taking either side would have punctured her dream.

Klara slept through it all. Thank heavens for Rosey, as solid as a brick.

"Maisy's right," she said. "She didn't agree to do anything else. If you can't announce right, you shouldn't have the megaphone."

Cilla held her ground. "It's not my fault," she said. "You all told me Maisy was a trick roper. I thought you knew what you were talking about. A trick roper does tricks. Spinning tricks. If all you do is catch, you're not a *trick* roper, that's called a *fancy* roper. How was I supposed to know that none of you knew what you were talking about? Don't you ladies know nothing? Do I have to teach you everything about being a REAL cowgirl?"

Her words stung. No one answered.

"I thought so," said Cilla. "It looks like I saved you from perpetuating an embarrassing mistake. What if we went all around the west, claiming we had a trick roper, and it turns out that all we had was a fancy roper after all? Oh, sure, some people wouldn't know any better. But the others, the ones who knew such things, the ones who'd seen Buffalo Bill's show and compared us to them, they would know, all right. Oh boy, wouldn't we look stupid then. So you see, I didn't make Maisy look bad. I saved her from looking a fool in the future."

Lill shrugged. "I guess it is better that it came out early."

"Your darn right it is," said Cilla. "And another thing -- Rosey's not a cow 'wrastler'. The official term is cow dogger."

Rosey frowned. "That don't sound right for what I do. Dogs is stupid little things. I don't even like them."

Cilla huffed, exasperated. "You should know the terms for what you do. Have pride in your craft. People have expectations. You owe it to them to get it right. You can't just go around making things up."

"There is a lot we don't know," said Lill. "Good thing we have you, Cilla, to steer us straight."

"She's steering us in circles," I said. "Trying to tangle us up. I wasn't the only one she tried to make look a fool. She's the one who told the crowd that Violet's first shot was a mistake. Cilla tried to get the folks riled up against her. 'Do it again,' she said. I heard her say it, clear as a bell."

"Are you sure?" Lill asked.

"You better believe it. I saw her hiding behind a tree when she said it."

Cilla frowned. "If I was supposedly hiding behind a tree, then you didn't really see who it was, did you?"

I didn't know what to say. She'd talked me into a corner, and I was stuck there.

Lill said, "Maisy, you were very far away. I couldn't see that far away."

"But I heard it," I said. "I heard it was her. I hear better than most. Like when Klara threw the candle up. It wasn't her idea. Violet told her to do it. I heard Violet say that, and they were even further away from me that Cilla behind the tree."

All eyes went to Violet, quietly scrubbing the pie dish she'd used for a fry pan.

She put the dish down. "Yes, that's true enough. I told Klara to throw the candle up, because the wick was getting so short. I was afraid it would burn her fingers."

Cilla shifted nervously on her feet. *Go ahead,* I thought. *Try to wiggle your way out of this one.*

"Maisy's right," said Cilla. "I did say that Violet should shoot it again. But not to set folks against her. I wanted Violet to show off what she could really do. And she did. Sure, I got the crowd stirred up. Stirred up *on our side.* And they loved it, that she kept shooting the flame right out. The more she did it, the more excited they got. But Violet, you can't decide willy nilly that you don't want to shoot the flame out of Klara's fingers. We had a schedule. A program to stick to. If you're going to change things, you've got to clear it with Lill and I first. We're the ones announcing what you do. This is exactly what I'm talking about. We can't just go out there and make things up on the spot."

Violet looked down.

"Cilla's right," said Lill. "We all owe her an apology. Thanks, Cilla, for keeping us on track. Ladies?"

Rosey and Violet mumbled some half-hearted thanks.

Cilla looked at me, waiting for me to ease down.

Not likely.

"Let's talk about making things up," I said. "What kind of trick did you do?"

"My horse is a registered trick horse," said Cilla. "I thought I told you that before, but I guess you don't know what it means. It means that whatever trick I do on my horse is registered, too, since he is. That makes it official. Recorded. Written down in some big book along with his name, and my named with it. Passed down from generation to generation, from every registered trick rider there ever was, to every one there will ever be, forever and ever. It don't get any more official than that."

It was either the most impressive excuse I'd ever heard or complete hog wash. If I was a gambling girl, I know where I would have placed my bet. But still, it left a sliver of doubt that maybe she was right.

"I guess we got that all cleared up," said Lill. "Cilla, why don't you go out and feed the horses. You too, Vi. I think Maisy should stay, so she can help me finish cleaning up in here. And Rosey, you stay, too."

It wasn't an invitation, it was an order. Although we were a democratic lot, with votes for the big things, the truth is that not all cowgirls are equal. By the way Vi and Cilla flushed out of there, and Rosey and I stayed, it was clear to us all that in the pecking order of our little group, I was the trouble-maker. And Lill was definitely the head hen.

THE SHAPE OF TRUTH

- 14 -

Ten minutes later, Rosey and I were out of there, too, off to the Owens' well to bring back buckets of fresh water. It was punishment, of course, and although I didn't mind hauling pails, I didn't like getting chewed out by Lill. I hadn't felt like this since Mama washed my mouth with paste so the poems she wanted me to memorize would stick.

"I'm not trying to mess everything up," I told Rosey. "I'm just trying to warn everyone. Cilla's up to no good. Why can't Lill see that?"

"Let it go," said Rosey. "It ain't worth the worry."

"How can I?" I asked. "Am I supposed to just let Cilla walk all over you and me, and Klara and Violet, too?"

Rosey shrugged. "To be honest, I don't know why you're so hot about Cilla. If there's someone you were sore with, I would have thought it was Violet."

"Why would I be sore at her?"

"Because of the way she dresses. Like she's too good for the rest of us, with her long skirts. And all that talk about finding a man. Has she got cotton for brains?"

I thought about that. In some ways, Violet was a lot like my mother. But there were differences, too. Important ones.

"Violet doesn't pretend to be something she's not," I said. "I respect that. What I like best is that she doesn't push her ways on anyone else. Heck, the only thing she pushes on us is food. And that's fine with me."

"That girl can cook," Rosey had to agree.

"But with Cilla, what she says and what she's thinking are two different things. I know it. I can smell it."

Rosey looked at me funny.

"Look how she talks," I said. "And the big way she brags about herself. But when it's her turn out there, well, you saw what happened. You were there laughing just as hard as I was. Remember?"

"I remember this," said Rosey. "We were ready to take on Klara, when we thought her cow riding was a joke. It was worth it, if we got a sharp shooter along with the deal. Lucky for us, Violet was as good as Pete said, and Klara was better than we thought. So what's the difference with Cilla? What if her tricks aren't so good? The rest of us can carry the show. Who knows? Maybe she'll learn."

"It's not the tricks that worries me," I said. "It's the way she fights against us. She digs little holes from beneath us so we'll fall on our faces. She does it so sneaky. That's what I don't trust."

"You're reading it all wrong," said Rosey. "I was mad at her, too, for a while. But the way she explained it, I'm inclined to believe her, that everything she's done has been for the good of the show. Remember, like Lill said, the show was Cilla's idea from the start. We owe her for that. Think of it from Lill's point of view. You know how bad she wants this cowgirling life."

"I know. But I don't know why."

Rosey looked down, as if debating if she should say any more. When she spoke again, her voice was low. "You'd never know from her smile, but Lill hasn't had it easy. Her Ma was a dance hall girl up in the Horn Mountains. Danced for money. Did other things, too. Lill was one of those things. She's never been proud of how she began and left as soon as she could. Now Lill's trying to make something of her life. Trying too hard, maybe. But you can't blame a gal for trying."

Once she'd said that, all the little pieces that made up Lill -- the crazy speed riding, the string of jobs, the shameless bawling in Pete's bar -- it all made sense. For Lill's sake, I wanted to like Cilla. I really did. But there was one more thing that bothered me. One last nagging issue that had to be put to rest before I could put it behind me.

"Why didn't Cilla want Vi and Klara to join up with us?" I asked Rosey. "She wanted to vote against both of them."

"That's not what I recall," said Rosey. "Cilla did ask for the vote. But she didn't vote against them. No one did that."

"But she wanted to."

Rosey shook her head. "Maisy, maybe you hear things from far, far away. Things that nobody else can hear. Maybe your hearing is super special. But as good as it is, there are things that even the best ears in the world can't catch."

Of all the people I'd ever met, I did not want to argue anymore with Rosey. I thought too much of her for that. And I sure didn't want to mess up Lill's dream. Besides, who was I to think I was some expert on human nature? Up until that point, there were only two people I had ever known very well. Meanwhile, Rosey and Lill were both older than me, Lill by a few years and Rosey by at least ten. They both had much more experienced with dealing with people. Maybe I wasn't right about this after all. Maybe I was just being like my Papa. Stubborn.

"What things?" I asked Rosey. "What is so impossible to hear?"

"You can't hear what a person didn't actually say."

*

By the time Rosey and I got back with the water, Klara was awake and had eaten her breakfast. Vi and Cilla were back, too, rolling up their blankets and packing their things.

"We're leaving?" I asked. I knew we couldn't stay forever in that tiny little shack. Still, it was the first "home" of the Darlin's, and the place we celebrated our first success.

"We've got to move on before it gets cold," said Lill. Of course she was right. On a bright August day with the clouds still fat with fluff, it was easy to ignore that the leaves were already starting to get brittle and dry.

Cilla added, "We should just have enough time to get to the Oregon coast before winter sets in."

"Oregon?" said Lill. "We're going to Denver."

"Why would we go there?" said Cilla.

"To find Buffalo Bill," said Lill. "Wasn't that the plan? Didn't you say we should form our own show and make our acts so good that old Bill couldn't turn us down? So now we've done it. Let's go show him how good we are."

"We don't have to have to do that right now," said Cilla. "There'll be plenty of time to catch up with him later. I thought, seeing how this is a wild west show, that we would take the show west. It only makes sense."

"That don't mean we have to go west," said Lill. "Pawnee Bill's show was in the east – all the way to Ohio. And he did very well there."

"But we're practically to the trail," said Cilla.

"What trail?" Rosey asked.

Cilla shook her head, disgusted with us all. "The Oregon Trail, of course. The path the settlers took when they made their way west. We have the chance to take our show on the same route the settlers took. To ride right over their wagon ruts. If you want the real *wild west*, what could be more wild and west than that?"

"But Buffalo Bill's getting old," said Lill. "I heard talk he was going to do a Farewell Tour. We got to get to him soon, before he retires. Or... or..."

Cilla laughed. "You think Buffalo Bill's going anywhere? You think that man's going to leave us? He's a legend. A rock. Ain't nothing going to happen to him. And to tell the truth, he's been doing his Farewell Tour for years. It's a publicity stunt. Gets people anxious to see him, that's all. Trust me, he'll still be doing that Farewell Tour long after we're as wrinkled as prunes."

That made sense to me. After all, he wasn't just a man, he was terribly famous.

"This is important," said Lill. "We have to vote. I say we go east, to Denver."

"And I say west," said Cilla. "Violet? What do you say?"

Vi shrugged. "I don't care which way we go. As long as we pass through plenty of towns, with plenty of men. Klara?"

Klara tilted her head. "My parents wanted to see the Pacific Ocean. They wanted to see the sun go down in it, like a sea of fire. I would go west."

"That sounds exciting," said Rosey. "I'll say west, too."

"The sun don't go *in* the water," said Lill. "It sets behind it."

Rosey looked confused.

Cilla shook her head. "Rosey already voted her mind. And once you vote, you can't change it. Maisy? Your turn."

In my mind, I could see roads stretching out both ways. Yes, the road east led to Denver and Buffalo Bill. But that direction also led to Pennsylvania and Mama. But I remembered that Cilla wanted to go west.

"East!" I said.

Lill looked relieved. "That's another vote for the east. How many said west?"

"Three," said Cilla. "We win."

Lill looked crushed -- almost as miserable as when we learned that Buffalo Bill had left Cody, Wyoming. For a minute, I thought she was going to spout.

Violet must have noticed it, too.

"Wait," said Violet. "I haven't voted yet."

"Of course you did," said Cilla. "You voted not to vote. That's what you said, wasn't it? That you didn't care either way? So that was your vote. And like I said before, you can't change your vote once you make it."

I looked at Lill. She was thinking. Hard. This was something she wanted very badly. And of all of us, she was the only one with the clout to clean up Cilla's rules, invented on the spot just so Cilla would get her way.

I remembered the time Papa played chess with a neighbor. This looked like a game of chess, with Cilla and Lill on opposite sides of the board. *Come on, Lill*, I thought. *Take her pawn. Take her pawn and her king, too.*

But then, Lill just gave a little shrug. "The people have spoken. It looks like we're heading west."

I didn't understand it at first, why she just let it go like that. But then, I thought past the next move as Lill must have done. And I saw that if Lill had changed Cilla's rules, and let Violet change her vote, it would have been three against three. Then there would be bickering. Arguing. Lobbying. Maybe even trading off votes for favors, just like the politicians did.

And our cowgirling dream would become a tar pit.

I'll always respect Lill for that, that she didn't use her power for herself but for the good of the group. I made a vow with myself right then to honor what Lill wanted from me. For the good of the Darlin's, I promised myself I'd try to go easy on Cilla. Even if it was the hardest thing I would ever do.

And it certainly would be.

OUT ON THE TRAIL

- 15 -

We didn't waste any time on goodbyes. We just packed up and got ready to ride.

There was no question about how much we could bring. We each brought what we could carry on the back of our saddle. I was used to traveling light, and Lill didn't seem to mind. Rosey, of course, had her own wagon so she could bring anything she wanted, which meant she could carry her tools. But Violet and Klara had things that didn't fit on the back of their horses.

We re-packed Violet's cooking supplies onto the wagon. There was cheese, butter, salted meat, and several sacks of flour. Enough to get us through several towns.

But they had personal things -- clothes, books, and a photo album -- that had to be left behind. They were not pleased about that.

Then we headed west. Due west.

Not southwest, the way most people went. Instead we traveled straight west. Cilla insisted it was the quickest way.

Our target was Montpelier, about 40 miles away. Cilla said it would take two days to get there. I suppose it would have if we were crows. But unable to fly over the trees, we got lost in them. We had no map and precious little sunlight filtering through the spires of the forest to guide us.

When you're traveling like that, you go as fast as your slowest member. Our slowest member was Violet's half-tail horse, Prize. Three miles out of Big Piney, it was clear Prize wouldn't make it carrying Vi and her personal gear. We loaded Violet in the wagon with Rosey, so Prize only had to carry the saddlebags.

Another mile later, it was clear that even this was too much for the old horse. We unloaded Violet's gear from Prize and put those things in the wagon, too. Still, with nothing on her back, Prize continued to lag behind. We bumble around in the forest at an agonizingly slow pace.

Rosey got testy. "Am I supposed to carry your horse, too?" she asked Violet.

Violet said, "I don't know why you would offer when we both know you're not strong enough." For a while, neither one said a thing.

After four days, when we still hadn't found a real trail, our meat and cheese ran out. Then the butter. Without shortening, the pancakes didn't fry well, so all we had to eat was burnt lumpy globs of flour paste.

Rosey got real mad at Violet for staving us, and Violet was mad back for complaining.

Even Klara and Violet didn't have two good words for each other, either. That was the only time I ever saw that pair at odds.

Then Lill got mad at Violet because Violet refused to shoot a rabbit for meat. Violet said she would never kill anything. It was a big moral point with her, and she wouldn't budge. So Lill snatched Vi's rifle away, and wasted a mountain of bullets not hitting a thing. All the noise spooked the horses until Rosey got fed up t and yanked the gun away from Lill.

That made me nervous because Rosey started making hungry looks at Klara's cow.

We were all mad at Cilla, who got us all lost in the first place. At least for once I wasn't the only one annoyed with her. Every once in a while she would blurt out, "It's not my fault that the stupid little town we came from didn't have a map store."

Cilla never took the blame herself, it was always somebody else's fault. Maybe that's what I didn't like about her. She had a big mouth but never took responsibility for the words that came out of it.

Then late in the afternoon of the 6th day, Lill caught a squirrel. This was not with the Violet's gun since Rosey had taken it from her. The squirrel was something Lill's horse Thunder trampled by mistake. Lill didn't see it happen. She heard Thunder snort, like he was disgusted, and then she saw the dead squirrel squashed under his hoof. We didn't know if it was already dead, maybe diseased, before he stepped on it.

Not that it mattered. We were too hungry to care.

We tied up the horses and made a big fire. I figured that squirrel would make about two bites for each of us. But Violet had other plans. She had Rosey pound some tin into a sort of baking box, which she put over the fire. Then using the squirrel's fat for grease, she baked it into a pie that smelled so good we couldn't wait to dig in.

It was a turning point for us. With our stomachs appeased, tempers eased. All the petty grudges didn't seem so important anymore.

The next morning the sun came up, shining a tiny beam of light through the trees. It fell on a path that led to a better trail than anything we'd seen in days. The trail led us out of that forest. In no time at all, we hit Montpelier. We thought we were saved.

We thought wrong.

A JAM IN MONTPELIER

- 16 -

Our usual plan was to stop at the outskirts of town and suss it out. But this time, we were in desperate need of supplies. Plus, Cilla insisted we should go into town. Her family, she told us, had come over the Oregon Trail. According to her, they'd practically invented it, and that the city was so grateful they erected a statue -- a great big monument to honor the Pystunia name. She said we'd be welcome, and was so persuasive, with tears in her eyes and everything, that we agreed.

It was late afternoon by the time we trotted down First Street, or maybe First Avenue. Whatever it was called, it was crowded with automobiles that poured fumes into the air. I had seen automobiles before, here and there, but never so many in one place. It was 1916, and in that town, there was hardly any horse traffic any more. Except for us.

The automobile drivers didn't like us, clogging up the street with our horses, slowing traffic down.

We rode from one end of First Street to the other end, but didn't see hide nor hare of the Pystunia family monument. It was only when we asked a shopkeeper on the far end of the road that we learned that that the Commemorative Oregon Trail Marker was on Third Street, not First.

We cut over to Third Street and headed back towards the city center, trying, without luck, to stay out of everyone's way.

It was Klara who saw it after the rest of us had passed it. The commemoration was a plaque at the intersection of Third and Washington that said, "Old Oregon Trail, 1854 - 1906". There were no names of clans or anything else, just a little bronze plate with a handful of words.

"We came all this way for this?" said Rosey.

"Where's the statue?" said Cilla, looking around. "Why did they take it down?"

It didn't look like there'd ever been a statue, or anything else. There wasn't any room.

"Let's head out," said Lill. "We've got to get out of this traffic."

"There's got to be more," said Cilla. "If we just keep going a little farther..."

Without warning, Cilla took off on her horse into the heart of the traffic, and wouldn't come back. We had no choice but to follow her down that street again, full of cars honking and tooting at us. Just as we were crossing the road, in single file with Prize dragging along at the end of our line, I heard a clunk and looked back to see what had fallen.

It was Prize. She was flat on her side on the street, staring up with eyes like wet stones. She'd dropped dead right there in the road.

It was that sound that haunted me for a long time. One minute she was plodding along behind me, then with the thud, she was gone. Just a scabby patchy scrawny lump of horse flesh, with those dead eyes staring and her pitiful wisps of mane fluttering in the breeze.

I yelled for a stop. We bunched up in the road, unsure what to do.

Our nerves were frayed, tired of fighting car traffic, sick from breathing exhaust fumes. In our defense, I will say that these things do not contribute to thinking straight.

"Just leave it," said Rosey. "We'll take the bit and the harness. The carcass can stay where it fell."

"We can't," said Violet.

Lill said, "Don't tell me you were attached to that bag of bones."

"It's not that," said Violet. "It's just that... that Klara and I sort of took these two horses, when we ran away from the fellow in Nevada. If he finds his missing horse here, with his brand still on it, he'll know where we are."

"You stole his horses?" said Cilla. "You two are horse thieves? I knew there was something fishy about you."

"We didn't steal them," said Klara. "We just borrowed them. He can have that one back."

Cilla turned on Klara, as if everything in the past week was all her fault. "How dare you?" said Cilla. "You've ruined everything! Even my family history has been wiped out, and I can't go retrieve it. All because of you!"

"Rosey," said Lill. "Can you haul that horse out of here?"

"It's too heavy to put in the wagon," Rosey answered. "I'd have to chop it into pieces, and dump everything else out."

The thought of holding up traffic for an hour or so while she hacked the dead horse into pieces, and then leaving behind our tools and Violet's cooking gear did not sound good to any of us.

We looked at the dead horse, and the angry cars honking around us.

The solution, crude as it was, was Lill's.

"Cut off the brand," she said.

"Here?" Rosey asked. "In the road?"

"You got a better idea?"

None of us had.

Rosey looked at me. "Maisy, you take the wagon and drive like hell. Leave me your horse and I'll butcher this brand off her."

I had only driven the wagon once, and that was on a dirt road with no traffic.

But I surely didn't want Rosey's job.

I untied Spackles and climbed into the driver's bench. Violet sat beside me three shades of red. Embarrassed, ashamed, and trying to hold back the tears at seeing the only horse she ever had get such a disrespectful send-off as this.

Big Red didn't appreciate my hands on the reins. Horses are skittish by nature, especially in traffic, and he wasn't pleased to leave Rosey behind. We hadn't gone far before he fell into a panic. I could barely control him as he galloped towards a whole line of cars. We were too close. The wagon clipped the side of one, sending sparks shooting out. Sugar, tied to back, slipped and kicked another one, crumpling the side like a sheet of tin foil.

We veered and skittered out of that town, and didn't stop until well after we'd left it.

We camped in the moonlight, far from that town's borders. We never again talked about that place or what had happened, even when Rosey finally found us late in the night, her hands red and sticky.

She spoke very little, and we didn't ask her. The only thing Rosey said that entire night was something I already knew.

"Maisy," she told me. "Your horse is a nag."

SODA SPRINGS

- 17 -

A day and a half later, just outside Soda Springs, I woke to the morning rays of sun burning off the gray clouds of dawn. It was a new day and a new town.

As usual, Lill's blanket was empty, always the first one up before everyone else. She wasn't in camp, and Thunder was gone. They did that together sometimes, a morning run as fast as he wanted. I wondered if Lill had gone back to town to listen for rumors, about a wild band of cowgirls with a littering debt.

After a while, I heard Black Thunder in the distance. I always heard him before I saw him, this time far off to the north, a soft rumble that steadily grew stronger. The sound of his gait was unmistakable. No other horse ran that fast. I walked to the north edge of our campsite and waited for Thunder and Lill to come into view.

A few moments later, Lill appeared over the horizon just where I predicted. She was wearing her usual furry chaps and her smile. I was glad to see the smile back. I didn't realize how much I had missed it.

She rode up to me and then hopped down off her horse.

"You always know where I'll be coming from," she said.

I didn't need to answer.

"I wish I had your ears, Maisy."

"I wish I had your speed."

She laughed, then pulled two things out of her saddle bag and passed them to me. "Give these to Violet," she said. "She'll know what to do."

I looked them over. One was a tin of butter, the other a little wood crate of comb honey.

"This town ahead," she told me, "it's a good one. Not too big, not too small. Just right, and ripe for our *pro-fessional* career." She said it so proud as she brushed sweat from Thunder's glistening black hide.

I took the butter and honey to Violet's blanket tent. She was half-asleep but she perked up when she saw what I had.

"From town," I said. "Lill got it."

"Hallelujah," she said. Then she sniffed the honey. "Pollinated from acacia nectar. This will be good."

I couldn't believe she could tell the exact plants the honey had come from, just by a sniff. Violet really did know her foods.

I went to check on Spackles, tied up with the other horses. Klara's cow was there too, right where we left them. But there were an awful lot of tracks in the dirt. More, it looked like, than Lill's taking Thunder out for a ride should have made. I couldn't tell for sure, but it seemed like the tracks went around and maybe even through our campsite. Could one of our horses gotten loose? I checked their lead ropes, but they were all tied on, each knot intact. It didn't make sense. Who had made the mystery hoof-prints?

Then a terrible thought seized me. Was it Prize coming back to haunt us?

Of course that was childish, and I was a grown woman, mostly. Still, I couldn't shake the lingering feeling that while we slept, someone, or something, had been watching us.

I went to find Lill. Rosey had a good fire going, and I forgot my question as I joined her, watching Violet do her magic over her grill. It was huge what difference a little butter made to the pancakes that morning, fried to a golden crust. The honey melted into them like liquid gold, and we ate and we ate until we were practically sick.

"I've been thinking," said Lill as we sat there, too full to move, "that this is a big occasion, what with getting ready to put on our first show since Big Piney. I think we should do something special."

"Get moonshine for a toast?" Rosey asked hopefully.

Lill frowned. "You would think of that. No, I mean something for the show. Something to kick it off. Something... I don't know... grand."

"Maisy's going to make a banner," said Cilla. "With *Little Darlin's* in big letters. When we ride out, they'll know exactly who we are."

"Like that," Lill said. "But more."

"We can start the show by praying," Violet offered. "After we come out with the banner, we can all get in a circle and hold hands and give thanks. We can shout it out so they know that we mean it."

"You are not religious," said Klara.

"Not yet," said Vi, "but it's not a bad idea. Menfolk like to see ladies respectful of those things."

It was such a bad idea, we didn't even have to waste time shooting it down.

But it got me thinking. What could we do to make our show really stand out?

"I saw an Indian ceremony once," Rosey said. "The chief's daughter wore a white deerskin dress with colorful beads. They said she was a princess. That looked special."

"I saw a princess once," said Klara. "In a parade in Germany, when I was a child. The dairy princess. We could do that. We could have our own princess."

A cowgirl princess. It made sense to me.

Lill smiled. "More than a princess, we need a queen. The queen of the Little Darlin's."

"Yes, yes!" cried Cilla. "With a scepter and a crown. I'll do it. I'll be a wonderful queen. A magnificent trick-riding queen!"

I couldn't believe her nerve. Did she really have no idea how awful she was? But I held my tongue. I'd made a promise to Lill to be nice.

Still, I had to say something.

"If you hold a scepter," I said with a perfectly straight face, "you'll have to do *flag hand* the whole time."

Cilla looked mortified. "You're right. I didn't even think of that."

Rosey started to laugh. Lill glared at us.

Rosey switched her giggles into a cough. "Must have got some pancake stuck in my craw."

"No scepter," said Lill. "And Cilla, you can't be the queen for every show."

"But I called it," said Cilla. "I said it first. You all heard me. This is not fair. We need to take a vote. Who wants me to be queen?"

"We are not voting on this," Lill said with *that voice*, the one none of us argued with, not even Cilla.

I was glad to see that Lill was finally taking charge, keeping Cilla in her place.

But part of me was disappointed we didn't get to vote that time. I knew Cilla would have been out-voted badly. I would have liked to see her deal with that.

"We'll take turns being queen," Lill announced.

"I like that," said Vi. "We can decide before the show. Make it really fair. Draw straws or something, so we all get a chance. Maisy, can you sew something special? Something that only the queen gets to wear?"

"A fancy headband," I said. "And maybe some special fringed gloves. Like what Buffalo Bill wears. But pretty."

Everyone thought that was a fine idea. Rosey drove me in the wagon to Soda Springs to pick up the supplies I needed to do that. Violet came, too, with a plate of honey-glazed pancakes to trade. Lill said I wasn't to take on any mending, since we were cowgirls now and didn't do scullery work.

But old habits die hard. When I got to town, I agreed to sew a few little odd jobs. I would see someone with a button about to fall off, and offer to fix it. More often than not, they would be curious enough to see what I could do. It wasn't hard, and it earned me enough cloth for the banner, a quarter hide of moose leather, and a huge fistful of beads. They glittered in the sun so bright that I had to squint, like a sparkly rainbow of color in my fist.

Maybe that's the problem with a beautiful thing. It's hard to look away. It can make you forget that all that shine and sparkle might distract you from something truly foul.

A CROWN OF FLOWERS

- 18 -

It was noon when Rosey got us back to the camp. I still had plenty of time for my projects. It was a nice feeling, to have nothing to do for a change but to sew pretty things. I spread my supplies on my blanket, planning the colors, enjoying the whole world of possibilities of things I could make.

Klara and Violet asked if they could help me. I let them watch. They seemed happy with that. Once I had planned out my designs, I cut out the shapes and let them sew the pieces together. They turned out to be reasonable stitchers, especially Klara. The beadwork I saved for myself, drawing out plump flower swirls onto each glove.

Rosey drove back into town with Cilla and Lill. They needed to sort out a field and a mean bull. That gave them a chance to talk up the show, and get the people excited about spending their money to see us.

It was late afternoon when they came back. By then the banner was done -- a length of stiff burlap with *Little Darlins* in yellow and white letters. The queening gear took longer, but was coming along, too, with pointy jags on the crown band and leather gauntlet gloves that flared up the arm.

Lill grinned when she saw how our work was shaping up. Rosey unhooked the wagon and came over to see.

"Roses on the gloves," Rosey said with approval. "Big ones, just like me."

"And violets, too," Violet added.

"How about lilies?" Lill asked.

"What about me?" Cilla asked. "My last name is Pystunia. Make some petunias!"

"Can you do it?" Lill asked. "Will they all fit?"

"Maybe not on the gloves," I said. "But I can add a whole mess of flowers to the crown. I haven't beaded that yet."

"Klara needs a flower name," said Violet. "Klara, what kind of flower do you want to be?"

Klara smiled. "I want to be Edelweiss. A beautiful flower that grows up high in the mountains where I came from. It fights the wind and the cold. I want to be a brave flower like that."

"You can't be Edelweiss," said Cilla. "It's not your name. It doesn't even sound like your name."

"But it does," Violet said quickly. "Klara's middle name is... Edelfina. Isn't that right?" Klara didn't seem so sure, but nodded anyway.

Rosey said, "Now we've got a flower for everyone. Except Maisy. That's a nick-name, isn't it? What's your real name?"

I shrugged.

They all looked at me.

I never liked my real name. Only Mama called me by my real name, and it sounded silly, to be named after a dead city. But the Darlin's weren't about to stop pestering me.

Finally I had to give in. "Macedonia," I said. "And you can just forget about my last name because there's no flowers named Lee."

"Macedonia Lee?" said Cilla. Then she started to chuckle. "No wonder you wouldn't tell us. Hardy, har, har. Our Maisy has a big, long, uppity name. So, how are you today, Maisy? Feeling... Macedonially?"

I stepped up to her, thinking how my knuckles would look jammed down her nose.

Rosey pulled me back.

"You don't need any of that," said Lill. "You've already got plenty of flower in your name. You can be our Maisy Daisy."

Klara tilted her head. "Daisy is a good flower. It grows where it wants. Six flowers on the crown. It will be like a garden."

"A garden of cowgirls," said Lill, "that's going to 'bloom' tomorrow at noon. Can you get it all sewed up by then?"

"Should be," I said.

Lill nodded. "We got the pasture and the bull. And a whole lot of people wanting to see us. They wanted to know all about the show, before we even said a thing. Maisy, Violet, what the heck did you say to those folks in town to get them all curious like that?"

Violet and I looked at each other. "I didn't say anything about the show," she said. "I just sold my fry-cakes. I didn't think they needed to know right away that I was *that* kind of girl. Did you say anything, Maisy?"

I thought about it a minute. I certainly hadn't made a big deal about it. I did meet a few folks. If people asked what I was doing in town while I was mending their buttons, I told them a little. But I didn't offer more than they asked.

"Maybe that's it," said Lill. "Maybe you said just enough to get them wondering about us. Like a puzzle, without giving away the secret too soon."

"Whatever it was," Cilla added, "you say the same things wherever we go. We'll send you and Violet into town. Get the people all warmed up, so that when Lill and I go in after you, the folks are dying to know all about us. Then, POW! Do I tell them!"

"She sure did," said Lill with a laugh. "I think we'll draw quite a crowd."

I was glad that Cilla's mouth, as loud as it was, was good for something.

*

I worked on the gloves and the crown well into the night, first by candlelight, then by the light of a three-quarter moon. Rosey told me I'd have time to finish in the morning, but I couldn't put it down. I never could sleep when I had a project to get done. As the last beads went on, I just curled up where I was and dozed off.

Sometime in the night, I heard a noise. A horse, probably, from quite some distance away.

It was too far away to be one of ours. Besides, I was too tired to worry about it. I would have forgotten about it, if I hadn't been reminded by what I saw when I woke up.

There was Violet cooking pancakes, as she often did. I expected to see Lill gone, off on her morning ride. But she was sitting with Rosey and Cilla, and talking to a stranger. She was a tall girl not too much older than me, with dirty clothes and a long snarl of hair the color of butter.

"Let me get this straight," Lill was saying. "You want to join us?"

The girl nodded.

"You can't be in the show," said Cilla, "unless you can DO something. You don't even have a horse."

"I don't have to be in your show," said the stranger. "I just want to come with you. I'll help out. I'll be useful. I'll do all the things you don't want to do."

"That's okay with me," said Rosey. "Sure. Come on along."

"Wait a minute," said Cilla. "She's not a cowgirl. We don't take stragglers. She can't come with us unless she's in the show."

"Fine," said Rosey. "Then she'll be in the show."

"She CAN'T be in the show," said Cilla.

"I'm confused," said Rosey. "You want her in the show or not?"

"I don't want her at all," said Cilla.

"I won't be no trouble," said the girl. "I'll work hard. Do whatever you say. Just please let me come with you."

"When did you get here?" I asked the girl. "Did you come to

our camp last night?"

"I tried," she said. "But something kept cutting me off. It was big like a horse. So I slept out there past that gully. It was gone when I woke up."

"What color was it?" I asked.

She shrugged. "I don't see so good in the dark."

Cilla snorted. "How can she ride with us if she can't even see? Besides, she don't have her own horse. Why are we wasting time with a stray? We've got a show to put on today."

"She don't need a horse," said Rosey. "Big Red won't even feel a skinny girl like her in the wagon with Vi and me."

"Eat first," said Violet, passing out plates of pancakes. "No one can think on an empty stomach."

Klara joined us. She had a talent for sleeping as long as she could, and waking up at the exact moment that Vi passed out the breakfast plates.

Violet handed the stranger a plate. She took it, sniffing the pancakes like they might be poison. Then right before our eyes, she chomped them down in a couple of gulps. It reminded me of when I got to eat proper food again, after living off eggs. I wondered how long this girl had gone without a good meal in her.

When we'd all finished, the new girl collected the plates. "I'll do that, she said. Then she started scrubbing them with a scratchy little weed.

We looked at her funny.

"Sage," she said. "A good cleaner. And it flavors your plates."

As she scrubbed the plates down, her shirt sleeve rode up her arm. I could see there were bruises, from her wrist up. They weren't fresh, they were old and fading. But the yellow mottled color told me they'd been deep.

"What in tarnation is all that?" said Rosey, never one to mince words.

The girl yanked her cuffs down. "I... ran into a tree." We all knew trees didn't leave scars on your wrist.

Violet and Klara exchanged a look. I knew what that meant. I'd lived with these ladies, with no walls between us, to know they'd seen this before. After all, they'd had man troubles, too.

I did a quick tally. With Rosey, Violet, Klara, and me ready to keep her, the new girl would get to stay.

"Vote!" I said, practically daring Cilla to challenge me. "Now."

"Wait!" said Cilla. She must have done her own head count, and came up with the same conclusion. "We'll take her, but only if she's got the right kind of name. As we were saying last night, all of our names have something alike. If her name doesn't fit..."

Rosey frowned. "You can't make up rules out of nowhere."

"I didn't," said Cilla. "We talked about it last night. Remember? We squared it up, and agreed, and Maisy put our special names on the crown. If her name don't fit, she can't stay."

We turned to the blonde girl. Lill said, "So, stranger. What's your name?"

The blond girl's eyes looked down, a little scared. Then she whispered in the meekest voice I ever heard. "Gloria. My name's Gloria."

"Too bad," said Cilla. "You got to leave. It's not me saying this, it's just that your name don't match with ours. It's not the right kind of name – it's not a flower."

"Sure it does," I said. "The morning glory. I've got room on the crown, in the back at the seam, for a blue morning glory with a squiggly vine. I'm out of beads but I can chalk it on, until I get more."

"Do it right now," said Rosey, "so she can be in the draw to be queen. All cleaned up, I'd say she'll be the prettiest one of us all."

If Cilla was mad before, Rosey's remark really fried her taters.

Lill wedged herself between Cilla and the new girl. "Glory, you can stay," said Lill. "And you will be in our show. You can march along with us when we ride in, and you can hold the banner. But you can't draw to be queen. Not this time around. Not 'till your flower is beaded onto the crown. Is that all right, Rosey? Cilla? Does that sound fair all around?"

Fair it was, though Cilla acted starchy. But she couldn't un-make her own silly rule, especially with Lill standing right there.

But it was her own darn fault – she had nobody else she could even pretend to blame. And as she stomped away, I think that's what bugged her most of all.

QUEEN OF THE SODA SPRINGS SHOW
- 19 -

Rosey took Glory to the hot spring to clean up while Vi, Klara, and I packed up the camp. Lill and Cilla sat off by themselves to plan the show, now that we had an extra person. They drew lines in the dirt to stage our grand entrance and map out the order of the show.

When Rosey and Glory returned, Glory looked like a different person. She was wearing one of Rosey's shirts and a pair of brown pants. With her skin scrubbed clean, it glowed peachy pink. And her hair, the tangles combed clean, shone like pure gold.

Lill approved, and said it was time. She took six blades of straw, mixed them up, and gave them to Glory to hold. That made sense, since Glory was the only one of us not in on the draw to be queen.

When I pulled mine out, I couldn't believe what a tiny little nub it was. I had drawn the shortest straw.

"Hail to the daisy!" said Lill.

"Our first queen," Violet added, smiling at me. "Seems only right, since you sewed the crown."

I felt a little embarrassed. It was just a leather crown and fringed mitts, for goodness sakes. I'd already put them on -- several times -- to make sure they were sewed right. To wear them again didn't seem like such a big deal.

But looking at that little straw in my hand, with the others so happy for me made my cheeks flush.

"Put on the crown," said Violiet. "With the daisy in front."

I turned it around so my flower was right above my forehead.

"That looks real nice," said Lill.

I felt nice, too, even though it was just cow hide with stitching and beads.

"If you're wearing the crown," said Glory, "I guess you won't be needing your hat. Can I borrow it?"

I didn't mind. So Glory took her corn-yellow hair, and bunched it up under my hat until you couldn't even see what color her hair was. Which, it seemed to me, was the whole point.

Then we mounted up, with Glory on Big Red with Rosey, and Violet riding on Lady along with Klara. Lill took off on Thunder to go ahead and collect the money before we got there. The rest of us rode to the show at a leisurely pace, a tidy little parade. Now we were seven, with five horses, one wagon, and an extra-wide cow.

*

At the field, a whole throng of people waited to see us. I saw Lill at the gate, waving her hat and wearing a smile that lit up that whole town. There must have been 160 people, at least. No wonder she seemed so pleased.

Glory and Violet walked into the ring, each holding one side of the banner, the letters hidden from view. The rest of the Darlin's followed on horse-back, except for me. I waited with Spackles outside the field, preparing for my royal grand entrance.

Glory and Violet faced the crowd, the banner between them, and flipped it around so you could read it. The others line up behind them. There they were, the LITTLE DARLIN'S, all clean and dolled up and as bold as our flag.

"Ladies and Gentlemen," Lill called out, her voice clear through the megaphone. "Preeeesenting, Miss Maisy Daisy, the QUEEN. Of the one and only ROOTIN'-TOOTIN'... ALL-GIRL... NO-MAN... LITTLE DARLIN'S WILD, WILD WEST SHOW!"

I slipped on my crown and gloves and rode Spackles into the

center of the ring. As the crowd cheered for me, Lill passed the megaphone to Cilla.

"You might be interested to know," Cilla called out through the megaphone, "that our very own queen, Maisy the daisy, is the great-great granddaughter of Washakie, the most famous chieftain of the Shoshone Tribe." The crowd gasped. It was news to me, too. I didn't even know who Washakie was.

The people seemed pleased and cheered even louder. I thought it was strange since I hadn't done anything at all yet.

But it did make me ride higher in my seat. Even Spackles seemed pleased, with an extra bounce in her step. As if considering for the first time that maybe humans weren't the root of all evil after all.

When the clapping was done, we went through the show in the same order as we'd done before. Lill blasted around with her speed riding. Violet shot her targets from Klara's hand. Klara rode her cow, and then Rosey and I brought down a bull that was big but not nearly as nasty as the last one we'd trussed up. This bull seemed kind of sad and pathetic, and I actually felt sorry for it. But the crowd was impressed.

When it was Cilla's turn, she did her flag hands again. In a way, she reminded me of that bull -- way out of her depth. I actually felt bad for her, too -- to want to be with us but have no talent worth earning it. Once again, the crowd was confused. And once again, when we started to clap, they joined in. Maybe they thought she was addled or blind or something, for us to be cheering her on like that. They were good people, to root for her. They didn't know her only handicap was her mouth -- it had a problem spouting the truth.

When she was done, the seven of us met in the ring, holding hands and taking our final bows. I was so full of good feelings I thought my heart would explode. I looked up in the sky and waved, so that if Papa was looking down from heaven, he'd see just what I'd become. A grown-up girl. With a life as exciting as anything I ever dreamed.

Not to mention a moose hide queen.

SCARLET DREAMS

- 20 -

Violet wanted to stay in Silver Springs until Sunday. She'd noticed some strong fellows in town and hoped to see them at church. But she was out-voted. With our first official show a success, we were eager to take on the next town. Besides, the way I saw it, after people had paid for our show, they didn't need to be reminded that Cilla wasn't impaired.

We loaded up and headed west along the south bank of the Snake River. This made Cilla happy since it followed the Oregon Trail. Not that we were doing it for her. In fact, we were all getting pretty good at ignoring Cilla's advice.

We skirted Pocatello. It was a big town, with more traffic than Montpelier so we gave it a miss. Two days later, we made it to American Falls. The noise of the rapids crashing down those rocks was so loud you could hear it a mile away. That pounding sound gave me a headache.

We got in late, too tired to go into town so we pitched our camp under the stars for the night.

My headache didn't go away, it only got worse. I checked if any of the Darlin's had mending. That usually got my mind off things. No one had tatters to repair, but Glory asked if I could make her something to hide her hair. She didn't mind holding the banner in the show, as long as every bit of her corn-silk hair was tucked away.

I didn't ask her why. I figured that was her business. With some left-over scraps, I sewed her a head-wrap and a hat. Then I went even farther, adding a fringe of fake black hair that I made from horse tail. I took just a little bit from each of our horses, mostly from the underneath side of the tail where it wouldn't be noticed. When I was done, from twenty feet, you'd have sworn that whoever wore that wig hat was a true brunette.

Still, my headache lingered on. It got so bad I didn't have the strength to show Glory what I'd made her. I pulled my Father's barn jacket around me tight and curled up into a ball. I wrapped my fingers around the hat I'd made so I'd remember to give it to Glory in the morning.

When morning came I could barely open my eyes.

"Quit stalling," said Rosey. "You're supposed to go into town with me and Violet."

"Can't," I said. "Just can't."

"What this?" said Rosey, prying the hat from my hands.

"For Glory," I said.

"Where'd you get the furry stuff?"

"Not fur, it's hair," I said.

"Whose? Wait a minute. You didn't..." Rosey stomped off. When she came back, she was fuming.

"Maisy, you should have asked," she said. "Lill will kill you when she finds out what you did to her horse. What you did to all the horses."

I curled up into a ball. "Can't kill me if I'm dead already."

A while later, Klara came over with soup. The new girl was with her, but I couldn't even remember her name.

"Where's everybody?" I asked.

"Rosey took Lill and Violet into American Falls, since you wouldn't get out of bed. Drink this."

I tried, but it spouted back up.

Someone put her hand on my forehead. Sometime later, they wrapped cool cloths on my head. They tried to make me take little sips of water, but even that was hard to keep down.

I knew they were upset, but I couldn't tell them not to worry. I couldn't talk or see them anymore. My vision was one big cloud.

All I could do was stew in my own sweat, and hear things, though I couldn't be sure they were real or not.

This went on a while, maybe days, with me shaking and shivering in my blanket, unsure where I was, or who I was. In my fevered state, I saw a man who made me drink syrup that smelled like bark.

I saw other things, too, but nothing seemed real.

I thought I saw Lill ride Thunder so fast that he sailed into the sky, and went higher and higher until they danced with the stars.

I saw Rosey wrastle a steer that shrunk into a calf, wet with afterbirth, and slid out from under her, running away as it bayed for its mother.

I saw a ring of flowers entwined by their leaves, with faces on them that were turned towards the sun. And a circle of tiny little horses beneath them, with their tails nipped off. Then all together, the horses fell over, as dead as old Prize.   Then a dark weed reached up from the dirt and choked the light out of the flower faces one after another.

After that, one more vision came. The night sky molded itself into a dark cloud, as gray as the dawn. It smelled like molasses. Like sweet feed. It stayed there all night, guarding me. Protecting me. Until at last it was chased away by the sun.

The gray cloud returned later. But this time it had a face. It was my father's face, looking young and carefree. He told me it wasn't my time. I wanted to stay with him, but he said I had to go back.

The next thing I knew, I saw Rosey and Cilla, in normal colors this time. They weren't all flowers and sunshine, like my vision dreams. They were arguing.

That was my first tip they were real.

"You don't get scarlet fever from a headache," said Cilla. "Not in the middle of the summer. She had to get it from someone."

"It wasn't Glory," said Rosey. "Or else she'd be sick, too."

"It had to be Glory," said Cilla. "She's the only person it could be. I told you not to take that girl in. I told you! And now Maisy is dying – she won't last another day, and it's all because none of you would listen to me."

"I'm not gone yet," I said.

"She's awake!" Rosey exclaimed. "Praise be, Maisy just spoke, as clear as a bell. It's a miracle!"

They rushed around me, and as I looked up, I could see all their faces washed in relief.

Maybe I was still a little foggy, but it seemed that Cilla wasn't as relieved as the rest. She seemed almost annoyed, that I woke up just in time for her to lose her debate.

I was glad to be back. Glad my headache was going out like the tide. I was pleased how happy my friends were to see me.

I was especially glad to have fouled up Cilla's argument, and foiled whatever plot she'd been hiding behind it.

I should have known there'd be repercussions. I should have known.

*

With the help of the Darlin's, I recovered. When I was back on my feet again, we put on a show in American Falls. This time, Klara got to be queen. I was glad to pass on the crown. I wasn't yet up to roping a mad bull, but I did rope a smelly billy goat. It was one of our best shows, I think. Maybe it was because of my brush with death, but that performance shines in my memory very brightly. Glory, in her dark wig, held our banner high and proud. Lill seemed to ride faster, Vi shot from farther away, and the sight of Klara bouncing along on the back of that cow, with her hair in braids under the beaded crown --

it was the most joyful thing I'd ever seen.

Even Cilla did something special. She did her double flag hand with a blindfold. Still not much of a trick since I think she was cheating, but at least it looked almost legitimate.

We made a little more money to add to our stash. But it wasn't as much as we needed because we'd burned through most of our food while they were waiting for me to get better.

Violet was striking out, too. She was learning that men are more slippery than fish, and a few Sundays in church was not nearly enough time to snag one for the long haul.

A GUARDIAN ANGEL

- 21 -

West of American Falls, we passed Massacre Rocks. Cilla told us horrible stories about what happened there, with whole wagon trains of settlers getting murdered by Indians. Until, she said, her grandaddy came along and saved the day single-handed, with nothing but a bull whip and a bent cavalry sword.

I didn't believe her. Not for a second. But that night as we sat around a campfire on the river rocks, our stomachs full from double helpings of Vi's beef dumplings with stewed greens, I could almost feel the old ghosts of Massacre Rocks.

It was Glory, who didn't even ride, that got us talking about a subject we had never discussed before.

"How do you pick your horse?" said Glory. "Do you find one that's just like you, or do you turn into twins after you've had it a while?"

"What do you mean?" said Cilla. "Are you saying we look like horses?"

"Not in the face," said Glory. "But haven't you noticed that all of you and your horses seem to match?"

"She's got a point," said Violet. "Look at Lill and Thunder. They live for speed. I swear, Lill, when you're riding full-out, in your black chaps, you and Thunder look like one single creature, with one heart and soul."

Lill smiled. "He is a pretty boy."

Klara nodded. "Rosey and Big Red. Big and strong. So dependable."

Rosey shook her head. "Big and strong, sure. But I don't let that horse off his tether. Last time he ran off, he lit out with some mares. It took me a week to find him and drag him back."

Lill said, "Remember that time Maisy and I have to rope you to drag you back from the bar?"

Rosey's cheeks turned as pink as her name.

"What about me?" said Klara. "How am I like Sugar?"

"You're not like your cow," said Lill. "But maybe your horse, Lady. She does her job. No trouble at all. Except when she bites."

"I do *not* bite."

Violet smiled. "Not after your second cup of coffee."

"Then there's me," said Cilla. "I'm a trick rider, and so is my horse!"

Lill nodded her agreement, though it didn't make sense to me. Cilla rubbed me wrong all the time. But her horse had no personality at all.

"This theory is all wrong," I said. "I am nothing like Spackles. She's stubborn. Quick to anger. And she has a way of letting you know she's mad even though she can't say a thing."

A hushed silence followed.

Finally Lill said, "You would never shoot fire with your eyes."

At once the rest exploded in laughter. I realized there was truth to it after all. I laughed with them until tears ran down my cheeks.

*

The next morning was misty and gray. I took a walk in the early dawn along the flood bank. There in the flats were clean tracks. Lots of them. Nearby was a little patch of white-tipped fur caught on a bush, spattered with red. I was no expert tracker but it looked like a fight. Two animals -- a horse with hooves and something with claws -- had been in a battle. The horse must have won, because the clawed creature had been run off.

This didn't make sense. Our horses spent the nights tied up.

The prints were fresh. So was the blood.

I went back to the campsite to get Rosey. If anyone could read these tracks, it would be her.

Rosey was still sleeping, so I had to wake her up. "Come quick," I told her. "Before they wash out."

Rosey didn't ask any questions. She extracted a knife as long as her arm and followed me. I knew she slept with a blade but I'd never seen in unsheathed. It looked as sharp as a razor.

Violet and Glory, who were starting the breakfast fire, saw us and followed. We got to the flats where the tracks were the cleanest. Rosey knelt to the ground, placing her hand on a print to measure the size.

"A coyote?" I asked.

"Too big for that," said Rosey. "Looks like a wolf. Probably a lone male. Chased away, tooth and nail... by a horse?"

"When?" I asked.

"Recent," she said. "It rained the day before."

"Who was it?"

"Had to be a big one," she said.

"Big Red?"

Rosie gasped. Then she took off up the bank, running to the clearing where we'd parked the horses last night. We all followed her there -- me, Violent, Glory. Even Cilla who heard us making notice and came along.

We got to the little clearing, and there were our horses, safely tied up, nibbling on leaves. Big Red was there, along with the rest. All except one.

"Thunder?" I said.

Rosey shook her head. "I 'spect he's out with Lill. Besides, his hooves don't match those prints. I should know. I shoed him."

"A wild horse just passing through?" Violet asked.

"Wild horses don't wear iron shoes," Rosey answered. "We only have two horses with shoes like that. It ain't Big Red. So it has to be..."

Rosey looked at Cilla.

"My trick horse," said Cilla. "He's got the big feet. So the old boy untied himself, chased some critter away, then tied himself back up. I guess it only makes sense. He is the only trick horse here."

I stared at Cilla's gray gelding, no expression on his face at all. He looked as dumb as a barn. It wasn't possible -- it made no sense. Horses don't tie and untie themselves. How could Cilla's horse possibly be smarter than all of us people and braver to boot?

Cilla patted her horse. "You tricky thing, sneaking off at night like that. But don't do it again. You do what I tell you from now on, and stay put. What am I going to do with you? You're a naughty old boy, Dusty Blue."

*

We went back to our campsite. Violet finished the pancakes and the morning resumed like any other.

But I just could not get my mind around what seemed to have happened. It just didn't make any sense.

"I don't know what you're all in a tither about," Rosey told me. "Everything's fine. We're all fine."

"But you saw it! You all saw the tracks."

"Just eat," Rosey said. "We don't want you getting a relapse."

I couldn't eat. I couldn't ignore it away. I took a plate, to please Violet, and waited at the edge of the campsite for Lill to return.

She had barely dismounted when I told her the news. Then I dragged her to the mud flat to show her the tracks. By then, the prints were already fading, and the fur patches had blown away.

"What's this supposed to mean?" Lill asked.

"It was here!" I said. "A wolf and a horse. There was a fight. Just ask Rosey."

"Calm down," said Lill. "Let me get this straight. You think Cilla's horse gets loose so he can chase away strangers and fight wild things?"

"That's what Cilla thinks. They were big hoof prints. Rosey says it couldn't be Big Red. But it has to be. It just has to be."

Lill thought a moment. Then she said, "No, it isn't Big Red. It's Dusty Blue. But he doesn't untie the rope. He slips his halter. You can see how he does it, with that big head of his with those little ears. It's true, Maisy. When I go out to saddle Thunder, Cilla's horse is standing there with all the rest. But his halter's on the ground. He stands there as if it was still on him. I didn't know he went anywhere. I thought it just fell off and he was too dumb to notice. So I put it back on him, nearly every morning when I take Thunder out for his ride."

I couldn't believe it. "You didn't tell anyone?"

"It's so early, nobody's up."

Things were starting to make sense. The mystery hero, the horse who kept Glory away, the one who would not let strangers enter our camp, was uncovered at last. Yet all this time, I hadn't given him any notice at all. I thought he was dumb as a cloud.

A gray cloud. Like the one I had seen in my fevered dreams, keeping dangers away.

There was only one way to be sure. I leaned into his neck, towards his long head with his eyes downcast, as if he'd done something wrong.

I sniffed his muzzle, and waited for him to exhale.

There it was, as clear as a frosty morning, that singular, distinctive smell.

Sweet feed!

THE RIGHTFUL SEAT OF CASSIA COUNTY
- 22 -

I asked Lill to keep it our secret. She agreed. No one seemed to care all that much anyway. But from that day on, when the sun breached the horizon, I woke up with Lill. After she'd gone off on Thunder, I'd ride Dusty Blue. I didn't use a bit or even a saddle. I just climbed up and let him go where he chose. I started to realize he was taking me to the places where he'd spent the night. It might be a hill or close view where he could overlook our campsite.

There I would see what he saw. A herd of deer off to the south. Or a moose cow with twin calves fording a creek. And for many miles, the mighty Snake River off to the north, coursing through the state like life-giving blood.

If I forgot and slept too late, he would come get me, and nudge me awake. He'd be back tied to his place with the other horses before breakfast, before the other Darlins were even awake. I didn't tell anyone about our morning rides. Not Rosey, not even Lill. It was our secret, and I liked it that way.

*

Our next town was Burley. I didn't go into town to do mending. The girls wouldn't let me. They didn't want me catching anything for a relapse. So while Cilla and the others went into town, I took little walks around our campsite. I noticed the tracks that I found. Now I knew those tracks told stories, often with Dusty Blue as the star. But I found other footprints, too. There were web-footed prints of the water birds. Tiny little paws of burrowers and diggers. The hooved prints of bigger game. I found I could separate the walkers and shufflers from the bounders, just by length of their gait.

The girls came back from town and told me we'd be holding our show the following day. Sometimes we parked a few days to feel a place out before scheduling the show, but Cilla was in a rush for this one. She didn't tell us why.

The next morning, it was Rosey who won the draw to be queen. She was excited at first, and put the crown on right away with the beaded red rose in the front. But the band was too small for her head and wouldn't stay on, so she passed the crown to Glory.

Cilla reached out and snatched it away. "Glory can't wear the crown," she said. "Not until Maisy sews on her beads. Glory's not official until then." It was true I hadn't yet secured more blue beads to sew on Glory's flower.

Rosey shrugged. "Then I'll pass my queening turn onto... Lill."

"You can't do that," said Cilla.

"Why not?" Lill asked. "Rosey won the draw. She gets to pick."

"You're only saying that because it's you that she picked."

"I'm saying it," said Lill, "because it's fair." The rest of us agreed.

So it was that the crown was turned to the white lily in front when we rode into Burley to show the good people what we could do.

*

We arrived to find the biggest crowd we had ever seen. There were 300 people at least, all gaping at us.

"Is this all for us?" Lill asked.

"It sure is," said Cilla with a grin.

"What the heck did you tell these people, to get them all here?"

"Just that we are the best. And they deserved the best, because they are the best. That's what I said. More or less." Knowing Cilla, that 'more or less' part worried me.

"The deal is," Cilla continued, "that I announce the show. Every bit of it."

Lill agreed. After all, since Cilla had whipped up all these people, maybe she deserved to officiate. Besides, being queen, Lill couldn't very well announce herself.

We paraded into the field and got into place. Cilla stood there front and center, enjoying the attention as all those people hushed for her to speak.

She whipped the megaphone to her lips and launched in. "Ladies and gentlemen. Here we are. Your All-Girl No-ALBION Little Darlin's!"

The crowd cheered like wild. But I had to wonder -- what the heck was an Albion?

"We're here in Burley," Cilla continued, "because Burley is the best. Burley is the greatest. Burley is the RIGHTFUL seat of Cassia County!"

Another cheer, this one louder than the last.

"And now," Cilla went on, "here is our queen, Lillith Geller, riding for you fine folks in Burley, the true seat of the county, and not that minuscule spec on the map called Albion, no matter what the county documents say."

More rousing cheers.

I vaguely remembered a signpost for Albion. Apparently, these people of Burley, a much larger town, didn't like playing second fiddle to their smaller neighbor.

These folks hadn't come to see us. They'd come to see cheerleaders for their cause.

We got through the show, but just barely. With Cilla announcing every single bit, things naturally went wrong. That gal just didn't know when to shut up.

The crowd cheered for Lill, but not because she was our queen. They thought she was the queen of the 'change the county seat' campaign.

When it was Vi's turn to shoot the candle out of Klara's hand, just as she pulled the trigger, Cilla shouted out, "Go, Burley!" Violet flinched, and if Klara hadn't instinctively ducked, she would have gotten her head blown off.

The crowd thought it was all part of the act. But we all knew better.

By the time I was supposed to rope the bull, I was so mad at Cilla I could hardly see straight, let along throw straight. This bull had sharp, lethal horns and my first toss missed by a mile.

"Come on, Maisy," Cilla called out. "Don't let us down. Do it for Burley. Do it for the RIGHTFUL HEIRS of the Cassia County seat!"

I threw my second toss and missed that one, too. As the bull continued to charge, I snapped my rope back. But he was too close, and I knew too well I wasn't likely to get this third toss off in time.

It was Rosey who saved me. Standing off to the side, she shouted, "Hey, bull! Come get me!" The bull noticed her and changed course to gore her first. That bought me the seconds I needed for the third toss. With Rosey in danger, I couldn't afford to miss.

I let my loop fly and nabbed him, all right. He looked mad to be roped. Just about as mad as I felt.

Rosey was flaming angry, too. She shook her head and walked off the field. I dropped my rope and followed her out. We couldn't cotton to Cilla's nonsense one second longer.

I didn't hear what Cilla announced after that. I do recall her out in the ring, waving and throwing kisses to the crowd. She didn't bother with her trick riding that day. Why should she? She already had the crowd's support.

Then she signaled for us to come out for final bows.

Rosey and I didn't go. None of us did. We were protesting the whole thing.

Cilla didn't mind having all the bows to herself. Basking in her moment, she mounted Dusty Blue for a victory lap. But being such a poor rider, she yanked too hard on his reins. I could see it had to be painful on his mouth, but he didn't grumble at all. Now that I knew this horse, I understood why. Cilla was a horrible thing, and he was smart enough to know that. But he also knew she was his owner, so it was his job to put up with her, without complaint. So he did.

If I hadn't found those tracks, I would have thought he just was as dumb as she was, and never realized what a brave, clever, thoughtful creature he was.

I realized I had underestimated Cilla, too. She had one serious talent after all.

She was an exceptional liar.

CILLA MAKES HER POINT

- 23 -

When we got back to our campsite, Lill was already there, her things rolled up and ready to go. It didn't take a genius to see she was hopping mad, too.

As foolish as Cilla was, she had the sense at that moment not to say anything. Instead, she faced Lill, the two of them locked in some kind of stare-down while the rest of us tried to make ourselves busy anywhere else.

Then Cilla tossed a leather pouch down, right at Lill's feet. It landed with a jangle and money spilled out. There could have been a hundred dollars in there with all those coins.

"You might not like how I did it," said Cilla, "but look what we made. For the Darlin's. For the good of the show."

Lill looked down at all that money. Rosey frowned and looked away. I knew what was on her mind. She was hoping Lill would tell Cilla what to do with her pile of coins and give her the boot.

But for the first time, I wasn't hoping Cilla would go. Because if Cilla left, she'd take her horse with her.

Dusty Blue looked over at me, his big eyes droopy, as if he was reading my mind. He seemed to understand important decisions were being made.

"Fine," said Lill to Cilla. "But you are never announcing again."

Lill got on Thunder. Cilla mounted Dusty Blue. They left that sack of money on ground and rode off in different directions.

Rosey shook her head, unhappy Cilla got to stay with us. She hitched Big Red to the wagon. She wasn't going to touch that money, either.

For a moment I wasn't sure what to do. That bag of money could buy us a lot of cowgirling. But were we all too proud to bend down and get it?

It was Glory who picked it up. She scooped up the coins and stuffed them into the bag. Then she loaded it, and her things, into the back of the wagon. She'd told us that first day that she'd take care of those chores nobody else wanted to do.   That's when I knew she was a gal of her word.

*

We passed through some small towns, Hansen and Kimberly and Filer, and Cilla behaved herself -- restrained and unboastful. She hardly said a thing. The quiet Cilla was much easier to take.

I wondered how long it would last.

We put on a show in Twin Falls. Cilla didn't go into town beforehand, but just stayed at our campsite, not saying a thing.

The show itself went all right, with Lill announcing and no nonsense this time. We needed a good show, to get our confidence back.

But it was the smallest crowd we ever had. Apparently, without Cilla's mouth, bragging all over town, it didn't matter how good we were if nobody came.

Later that night, just west of Twin Falls, we camped out on a flat grassy patch not far from the Snake. I could practically hear Rosey's thoughts. *I risked my neck to wrastle a grown bull for twelve people?*

But of course, she didn't dare say it. Not with Cilla lurking around, quiet as a cat, just waiting to pounce on the first one of us to complain about the pitiful turnout.

Violet said, "I shot all my targets tonight."

"I brought down my bull," said Rosey. "And Maisy roped it just fine."

We were quiet after that. They wasn't much else we could say.

It was Lill who finally broke the subject we'd been tip-toing around all night. She turned to Cilla and said, "Okay, go ahead. You might as well tell us what you're thinking. Just come out and say it."

"Why should I?" said Cilla. "Clearly, you don't need me advertising the show. I might say the wrong thing. I might get too many people to come. I might make us too rich and too famous, and then what would we do?"

"All right," said Lill. "I'm sorry. We do need you. There is no show without you. At least, there's nobody to watch it without you. You still don't get to announce. But we do need you to talk it up in town. Just... next time, don't go so far."

Cilla smiled like the cat who stole the cream. Then everything went back to normal again. Cilla acted all full of herself. But now it was worse, because we all knew we needed her mouth.

Just after supper as Glory, Klara and I were putting away the tin plates, Cilla said, "I've been thinking. I've had a lot of time to do that lately, and I think Glory shouldn't wear that wig in the show."

"I like the wig," said Glory.

"But your hair's so bright," said Cilla. "As striking as General Custard's. As distinctive as Buffalo Bill's. Maybe we should call you Buffalo Betty. People would get a kick out of that."

"I'm wearing the wig," Glory said.

This went on a while, with Cilla pushing, and Glory saying the same thing back. Finally Lill said, "For Heaven's sake, Cilla, leave it alone. If Glory wants to wear that horse wig, it's up to her."

That shut Cilla up. But just as Rosey doused the campfire with a pan of water, sending a rush of sparks up towards the stars, I saw

Cilla's forehead wrinkle up in a way I couldn't forget.

A GIFT HORSE

- 24 -

With Cilla unmuzzled, we got our crowd back. The next show, in Buhl, went just fine. That is, until the very end of the show when we stood in the center of the ring to take our bows. We were all holding hands, with me next to Cilla and Glory just past her, enjoying the applause. Enjoying our fame.

All of a sudden, Cilla seemed to trip. Her hand slipped from Glory's and knocked that wig hat right off Glory's head.

At the sight of Glory's brazen blond hair, the cheering stopped dead. A moment later it resumed, even louder this time, with more whistles and hoots, all in the deep tones. The men tones. Glory was a fine-looking woman with her tall legs in those chocolate suede pants, even with a crude horse-tail wig.

But with her golden hair set free, the sight of her scrambling to hide it was the perfect picture, not only of beauty but modesty as well, and the men in the crowd just roared.

With the wig half on, she ran out of that ring and kept on going, not towards our campsite, but into the thickest tree cover around.

"Go get her," Rosey called to Lill, "before she gets lost."

Lill was off on Black Thunder before I could practically blink. The rest of us stood there, not bowing, just looking at the crowd that by now had started to break up.

"Come on gals," said Rosey. "Show's over. Time to go."

We got back to our campsite but Lill and Glory were not there. Rosey started a fire and Violet made a stew pot. Klara and I set out the plates to be ready to eat when they got back.

Then we waited.

The sun went down and the stew went cold, but still with no sign of Glory, Lill, or Thunder. I had the best hearing of any of us so I sat on a rock at the edge of our camp to listen.

An hour after sunset, I heard something.

"Are they back?" Rosey asked me. She could tell when my ears were twitching just by my face.

"A horse," I said. "But not Thunder."

Violet climbed onto the rock beside me. I pointed the direction to her. Her eyes were better than mine, especially at night.

With only a sliver of moonlight to see by, it took her a while to spot it.

"It's a man, looks like," she said. "He's walking a horse, not riding. Coming right towards us like he knew we were here."

"Why can't we eat without them?" Cilla wailed. "I'm starving."

"We're all hungry," said Rosey. "But we would have been full and washing the plates if it wasn't for you."

"What did I do?" said Cilla. "My hand slipped. I didn't mean to knock Glory's wig off. Besides, who knew she'd be so sensitive about it?"

"This is your fault," Violet told Cilla. "That makes it your job to fix. You talk to that man, whoever he is. Or else you get no dinner at all."

Cilla complained, but as our cook, Violet had control of the food. Grudgingly, Cilla went off to meet the man with the horse.

Just after she'd left, I heard hoof-beats coming from the east. Coming fast. "That's Thunder, for sure," I said. "But I can't tell who's on him, one rider or two."

Vi climbed back on the rock and cast her gaze east.

"Two," she said, relieved. We all felt lighter to hear that.

"I'll help re-heat the stew," said Klara. Rosey and I gathered firewood to help. We didn't care what happened with Cilla out there on the flats.

A moment later, Thunder appeared, bringing Lill and Rosey right up to the campfire.

"Where is she?" said Lill with a scowl. She didn't have to say who she meant.

Rosey pointed south. "Talking to some fellow out there."

Even by the campfire light I could see Glory turn pale. She started to shake, like a dry leaf in the autumn.

"Don't worry," Lill told her. "It can't be him. There's no way he'd get here that fast." Then Lill turned to us. "We need to eat," she said. "We'll talk later. When Cilla gets back."

Violet dished up our stew and we ate it luke warm. It was another twenty minutes before Cilla got back. We left her some scapings at the bottom of the pot.

"You saved the best part for me," she said. "All crunchy and nice." Somehow it didn't seem fair she enjoyed it so much.

"Listen up," said Lill in her serious voice. "Glory has reason to keep her hair hid. You don't need to know why, only that it's a good reason. If you don't agree -- if you don't PROMISE to help keep her hair under wraps..." Lill said glaring at Cilla, "then you can't be a Darlin no more, and you have to leave."

I'd never heard Lill talk so strongly before.

"I agree," said Rosey. Violet, Klara, and I all swore on our hearts to upholds Glory's wishes, too.

Only one of us hadn't agreed. We all turned to face her.

Cilla pouted. But finally she out, "Okay."

"Not just okay," said Lill. "This is important. You must *promise*. Swear on your life, Cilla. Swear on your word *as a cowgirl* that you won't ever tell anyone Glory's name or what she looks like."

"All right, I swear it," said Cilla. "But you're all being silly. That blond hair of hers is quite a draw. Why, just tonight some fellow came by to give Glory a horse. That's right. A nice palomino, with a beautiful buttery coat."

I couldn't have been more surprised if spiders had come out her mouth.

Rosey said, "I hope you sent him packing."

"Of course," Cilla grinned. "After he left the horse."

Glory turned white. "You accepted a horse in my name?"

Cilla nodded. "He's tied up with the rest of our horses."

I didn't believe her. Nobody gave away horses like that.

"Go see for yourself," said Cilla, looking very smug.

We all went to the grass patch where we'd tied up the horses. We found them resting, peaceful and calm. Even Dusty Blue, who hadn't slipped off his halter just yet. All of our horses were there.

And one more besides.

The new horse had a pale golden coat that nearly glowed in the moonlight. I had never seen a horse's coat shine like that.

"His name is Pal," said Cilla, "Because he's a palomino."

"I don't want it," said Glory. "You give it back."

"I can't," said Cilla. "The fellow's already gone."

"Are you saying," said Lill, "that some stranger gave Glory this horse? On account of her hair?"

Cilla nodded. "He said a gal like Glory should have a beautiful horse. His wife didn't need it no more -- I guess she died or something -- so he brought it here. He said it belonged with the pretty girl. It's not like he wants anything from you, Glory. Just a thank you is all. I told him you'd be happy to do that."

Glory was livid. "You had no right!"

Cilla shrugged. "You all told me to go out to that man and handle what he was after. So I did. We've been down two horses. Now we're only down one. You all should thank me. Why is it I have to do everything around here, but I get no appreciation?"

Glory didn't say anything. But her face got all puffy and redder than burning fire embers.

Lill shook her head. "You got no right to accept something for somebody else. It's not your place to do that."

"That fellow didn't mind," said Cilla. "So I don't know why you should."

"Take it back!" Glory shrieked. "I don't want it. Take it back!"

"She's right," Lill told Cilla. "Tomorrow, you go into town and give it back to him. I mean it."

"All right," Cilla said. But she rolled her eyes, just the same way Spackles did, that meant she didn't really agree.

*

We couldn't leave the next morning until Cilla came back from town. When she did, riding on Dusty Blue, she still had that palomino with her.

"Why are you bringing it back here?" Lill asked. "Couldn't you find that man?"

"I found him all right," said Cilla. "But he said if Glory didn't want it, I was just as fetching as she is, so I should keep it myself. So I am."

"You told him my name?" said Glory. "You used my real name?"

"No, I mean, I told him your name was... Jenny. I told him you didn't want the horse because you didn't ride. When he found out I was a trick rider, he said I could keep the horse for myself and use it for a spare."

That didn't make sense. With as much charm as a swarm of mosquitoes, who would give Cilla anything? But at the same time, I couldn't understand why a man would give a Glory a horse, either, no matter how pretty she was.

Lill agreed the horse could stay. But it made me wonder. There was a whole world of things I didn't know about people -- especially men. But I was beginning to know horses. It was clear Pal knew he was a beauty. While Glory worked hard to hide her good looks, Pal wasn't shy. He tossed his mane to catch every bright ray of the sun.

A DEVIL'S BARGAIN

- 25 -

From Buhl we took a detour south through the Salmon Falls
Canyon. There was a rock Cilla wanted to see, and Lill agreed.

It was late afternoon when we stopped to let the horses graze. I
didn't mean to listen in, but I heard Rosey talking to Lill.

"Why do you always give in?" Rosey asked her. "You let her
take us 16 miles out of our way to see a rock?"

"Not just any rock," said Lill. "It's the World's Famous
Balanced Rock. Since we are going to be the World's Famous Little
Darlin's, it makes sense to see it."

Rosey just sighed.

We came upon Balanced Rock just before it got dark. It was
certainly big, all forty tons of it perched above our heads. I wasn't sure
if it was worth an extra day of riding, but I did know that I was awfully
nervous standing below it.

"It looks like Africa," said Klara. "The entire continent
standing on its tip." I didn't know about that. I'd never been there.

Cilla said, "Let's camp right here beneath it!"

The thought of that made me feel ill.

"That would make us famous," Rosey said. "The World's
Greatest Squashed Cowgirls."

We picked our way down Salmon Falls Creek and didn't make
camp until we were almost back to the Snake. The next day we headed
west towards Glenns Ferry, where the early settlers had crossed over
the river to the north. We decided to cross the river there, too, since the
bigger towns ahead were on the north side.

"My granddaddy went over this river," Cilla told us. "On the ferry. Before that was built, he swam across with the wagons to save everybody from drowning. I just can't wait 'til we get to that ferry."

I wanted to see it, too. I had never crossed a river on a boat big enough to take horses. I knew Spackles wouldn't care. But Dusty Blue would appreciate it and understand what an amazing thing that was.

We got to Glenns Ferry the following day, and asked a woman with long loaves of bread where we were supposed to cross. She told us to go half a mile up the road. When we got there, we saw a long bridge that spanned the entire width of the river. It was wide enough for a wagon, and strong enough, too. We watched a farmer with a full cart of potatoes come over from the other side.

"Where's the ferry?" Cilla asked him. "The one they named this town for."

"There's no ferry," he told us. "Not since the bridge went up. Must have been eight years back. Don't worry, ma'am. It's plenty strong enough to support anybody. Even you."

Cilla gritted her teeth.

Rosey just laughed.

I didn't think it was funny. I could practically hear the argument coming. Cilla insisting we couldn't use the bridge since it wasn't a "natural" part of the trail. Rosey saying she should just jump in and swim. Cilla saying Rosey should swim over first, being the strongest, and pull us across. Then everybody would start talking at once, and nothing would get done.

I decided to head the argument off before it got started, so I went to the edge of the bridge and prodded Spackles with my boot to urge her on. She was surprised since we never took the lead.

I had to nudge her twice to show her I meant business. She paid attention this time and we rode across.

The rest of the Darlin's just watched us. A minute later they followed us over, no more fuss, no disagreement to launch into.

On the north side of the river we found a field for the horses to graze. I left Spackles there and walked into town with Lill. Near a shop that sold candy, a girl approached me. She was maybe 13 or so, with hair like marmalade.

"Are you one of *them?*" she asked me, her eyes as big as saucers.

"One of who?"

"The famous cowgirls! They say that they can shoot and trick-ride as good as any man. They say they can ride like the wind!"

I was surprised how fast news got around.

"Mostly true," I said.

"How big is your gun?" she asked.

"I don't shoot," I told her. "We all have one job. I rope."

"Could you rope that post over there?" She asked.

I didn't like to show-off, especially for free. But there was something about this girl, not much younger than me, that made me get out my rope. I twirled it up and lassoed that post clean.

Her eyes blew up like little balloons.

Just then, a woman with a black shawl and angry eyes called to her. "Don't dawdle, Angelique. Come here, now!"

The girl leaned towards me, her voice a whisper. "I want to be a cowgirl, too," she said. "Just like you. I want to go with you."

I looked at her face all eager and scrubbed clean. I wondered how she'd like living off raw eggs by herself. How she'd enjoy being lost in some forest with nothing to live on but burned flour paste.

I looked at the woman in the black shawl. I saw she was angry and harsh, but worried, too, about her girl.

"You be good," I said to the girl. "You listen to your Ma and have a good life."

The girl seemed crushed as I walked away. I started thinking about what I had told her. For the first time, I thought of Mama with some kindness. Did she still worry about me? Did she think I was dead, and arrange a lovely funeral, with all her big city relations crying for me? Was it wrong for me to leave her like that, without even a letter to let her know I was fine? After all, Mama had tried to give me what she thought was best. What she wanted for her own self. It wasn't her fault we didn't want the same things.

But it wasn't my fault, either. That was just the way it was. With us being so different, she would never understand me.

As long as I was far away, she didn't have to.

*

That night at our camp, as we watched the sun go down in a blaze of flame, I asked Cilla if she'd like to go for a walk. She looked at me sideways, but was curious enough to agree.

I was nervous. I had a big question to ask her. I wasn't good with words under normal conditions, and I knew I would have to get these words right.

She seemed to enjoy that I had trouble starting my question. Finally, I just let it out.

"Now that you've got two horses," I said, "with your new one so pretty, maybe you could sell Dusty Blue."

"He is getting kind of old," she said. "I've been thinking it's time for a horse who knows better tricks." Trust Cilla to blame her own failures on somebody else. "Why?" she asked. "You buying?"

"I'm thinking of a swap," I said. "I'll trade you Spackles for Dusty Blue."

"Why would I do that?"

"You said it yourself, he's getting old. Spackles has a lot more years left in her."

"She's no trick horse," said Cilla.

"No, but you told us you trained Dusty Blue. Just think of all the tricks you could do with two horses -- Pal and Spackles."

"I already have two horses," she said. "Why are you asking?

You must want him awfully bad."

It was true, but I didn't want her to know that.

"Okay," she said. "You can buy him for two hundred and fifty dollars."

It was an impossible amount -- more money than I'd ever seen.

But none of that mattered. The important part was that *Cilla had agreed.*

"Deal!" I said quickly, before she could change her mind. "It will take me a while to get it, but I will buy him for that."

"Not so fast," she said with a slippery little grin on her face. I didn't like that grin. "I wasn't finished. I meant two hundred and fifty dollars *plus*... the next time the Darlin's take a vote, you have to side with me."

"How can I agree?" I said. "I don't know what we'd be voting on."

"You want the horse? Those are the terms. I'm only asking you to vote my way once. Just the next vote that comes up. After that, you can vote whatever you please. Do you realize that every single time we've voted, you always voted against me?"

Of course I knew it. I was proud of that.

"Would it be so bad," she continued, "if just one time, you voted with me?"   I didn't know what to say.

"You're right about one thing," she told me. "Dusty Blue *is* getting old. If I don't find a buyer who wants him for riding, I might have to sell him for glue."   It was such a horrible thing to say, I couldn't help myself. "You can't!" I cried. "I want him!"

She shrugged. "Apparently, not very much, if you won't take my terms."

This had gone worse than I planned. Now Cilla knew how badly I wanted him. I didn't trust her at all. I couldn't put it past her to sell him for parts just out of spite.

My pride was on one side, with Dusty Blue's life on the other.

There was only one choice.

"Do you swear," I said, "never to sell him to anyone else, for any reason at all, even if it takes me a long time to get all that money?"

She said, "As long as you promise to side with me the next time the vote comes around."

We shook hands to seal the terms.

I felt good. Full of hope. I had something important to work towards. Nothing was going to stop me from saving up all that money. I was sure I could buy a good life for that horse.

A good life with me.

I was so happy I didn't see the problem.

If you deal with the devil, you are already sunk.

ROSEY'S TEMPTATION

- 26 -

The Glenns Ferry crowd was a good one. During the show I looked for the marmalade girl in the crowd. She wasn't there. I was partly relieved. If she could be talked out of cowgirling that easily, she didn't belong with us.

From there we cut north for a while, traveling away from the river until we came to a place called Mountain Home. I went into town with Rosey and Violet. We found two kinds of people there -- the usual rancher folks we met and a whole different type of people with black hair and dark skin. Rosey said they were Mexicans. They didn't mix with the others but stayed on their own side of town. They were friendly enough, but they did their own mending, and didn't need me.

That night while I was asleep at our campsite, Lill nudged me awake.

"Have you seen Rosey?" she asked.

I shook my head.

"I think she went into town," Lill told me. "You have to come with me. We have to find her."

"Can't it wait 'till the morning?" I asked.

"Not if she's gambling," said Lill. "I'll get the wagon. You bring your rope."

I was not happy about it, but I crawled out of bed and got a couple of ropes ready, just in case.

The night air bit me like a hundred little teeth, attacking every part of me that was exposed. I was chilled through and through by the time we found Rosey, at a boarding house with a bunch of people playing cards. It wasn't hard to find her. She was singing at the top of her lungs, drunk as a skunk.

Lill marched up to her. "We're taking you back."

Rosey laughed in Lill's face. Her breath smelled like kerosene, but more sour. Then she saw my rope. She seemed to deflate, and just followed me like a puppy back to the wagon.

Lill said we were lucky that the people Rosey was gambling with were Basque. Rosey didn't know how to speak that, so she hadn't bet too much away.

I drove the wagon with Rosey stretched out in the back. We hit a rock in the road that jarred her awake.

"She said she does," Rosey muttered. "She likes me. But not *like that*." Then Rosey gave a mournful sigh and passed out again on the wagon floor.

I looked over at Lill riding Thunder. "What is she taking about?" I asked.

"She don't mean nothing," said Lill. "She's just drunk. Drunks say things that don't make sense."

Just before we reached camp, I unhitched Big Red and dragged the wagon in. It was quieter that way. Nobody had to know what trouble Rosey had gotten into.

But at the campsite, I found Violet, Glory, and even Klara who slept hard -- all wide awake. Violet was holding her gun.

"Did you find her?" Glory asked.

Lill nodded. "She's fine. She just needs to sleep it off."

"She doesn't have any more liquor stashed away?" Vi asked.

"I will check," said Klara. "Who will help me?"

Up until then, I thought Rosey's drinking was a secret.

"I'm flat-out too tired," Lill said.

I was sure Glory would offer. I knew Rosey wouldn't mind Glory going through her pockets.

But Glory kept quiet.

I went with Klara to help check. We found an empty flask in

her boot and a half bottle of wine in her back pocket. It was a marvel the bottle hadn't broken. I would not have liked pulling slivers out from where it would have gone.

Cilla woke up and strolled over. She took one look at the bottles and said, "Why, you naughty girls. Having a party and no-one told me?"

At least she didn't know about Rosey's problem.

"We didn't want to wake you," said Lill.

Cilla frowned. "More for you, I imagine. Here. Give me that bottle."

Lill passed it to Cilla, who took a healthy swig. Then we all went to the campfire and passed it around.

I tried it, too. It was the first alcohol that ever touched my lips. It burned going down, but it warmed me up. It didn't taste anything like grapes. I took another swig, just to be sure.

Lill turned to Klara. "Does Violet always keep that rifle close?"

Klara nodded. "That man in Cheyenne was bad. He said if she left, he would find her."

Lill didn't say anything for a while.

Violet came over and joined us. Lill said, "I've never been east of the rockies. Tell us about New York. Do people really dance in the streets?"

Violet and Klara laughed. Then Violet started a story about going to a dance with her sister. The sister was sweet on some boy. The story went on and on, and I couldn't understand the point. Then right in the middle of it, someone interrupted and said, "I left my Mama. Before I turned sixteen. I just took off."

I realized with a shock that the words came from me. Somehow, the things I never discussed just tumbled out. It was as if the wine had unglued my mouth.

That stopped everything.

After a while, Glory said, "I ran away, too."

"My Mama tried to marry me off," I said. "To some sissy boy back east."

"That's nothing," said Glory. "I *was* married."

It was hard to imagine Glory, not much older than me, already a wife. I had no story to top that.

Cilla got a strange glint in her eye. "So, our two youngsters are runaways. No wonder you never talk about your past."

Lill said, "Ain't it something? Violet's always hoping to get married, while Maisy and Glory run the other way."

"I left because my Papa told me." I told them. "His heart quit and killed him. Then he told me to run. Twice."

"He actually said that?" Cilla asked.

I nodded. "I hear pretty good, you all know that. He said it so loud it woke me up."

Cilla started laughing. "He couldn't tell you anything after he was dead. Don't you see? You were just dreaming. The whole reason you ran away – it was just a mistake."

"But I heard him," I said. "Didn't you pay attention? That's your problem, Cilla. You don't listen to nobody else, you just jump right in and open your big fool mouth."

Cilla looked like I'd punched her. For a moment nobody moved.

Then Lill said, "Come on, Maisy. Let's get you to bed."

Lill and Klara helped me stumble back to my blanket. I smiled all the way, feeling pleased with myself. Roping and sewing were easy but I'd just done something I thought I'd never be able to do.

For the first time since I'd joined the Darlin's, I had out-talked them all. I was so pleased with myself I forgot the reason I stayed quiet.

BUCKING BRONCO RIDER REQUIRED

- 27 -

From Mountain Home, it was a straight shot to Boise. Boise had been a fort during the settler days so of course Cilla was dying to go there. The road was well-kept so riding was easy. But as we got close to the city, the road started to get crowded. There were people in wagons, people in automobiles, and people in trucks.

We decided to stop for an early lunch. We pulled off to the side and started a fire.

Lill talked to a farmer with a wagon full of peppers, hoping to buy some. As she bargained the price, the farmer, a tall gangly fellow with whispery tan hair, told us we shouldn't go to Boise, we should go on to Nampa. He said they held a harvest festival every year with a rodeo stampede. The vegetables grew huge there because it was the "banana belt" of the state.

Lill didn't understand how it could be warmer if it was just over the hill.

He didn't know why, he just said it was true. The more he talked, the more we all wanted to skip Boise.

Except Cilla. She was still dead set on Boise.

Lill said, "Let's vote."

I was ready for that. I'd be glad to vote with Cilla, like I promised. With the other four against us, we'd still end up going to Nampa.

Cilla figured it out, too, because she looked at me sideways. "No," she said. "We don't need to need to bother with a vote. Nampa it is."

The others didn't understand why Cilla gave in without a fight.

For me it felt strange, to have this secret power over her.

But I didn't give it much thought. I had other things on my mind. With the warm days of summer slipping away, Nampa sounded great.

Besides, I couldn't wait to see what Violet would make out of all those bananas.

*

When morning came, we had our breakfast and saddled up. We reached Nampa before noon. I was surprised how quickly we got there. It didn't feel any warmer than Boise, no matter how hard I tried to convince myself.

Once the horses were settled, I went into town with Rosey and Lill. There was no fruit on the trees and hardly none in the shops. As far as banana belts went, it was a real let-down.

A shop-owner told us we couldn't put on a show unless we got a public display permit.

I went to the city hall with Rosey and Lill to get one. We found the man, Mr. Stevens, in charge of issuing the permits. He was a round little fellow hunched over a tiny desk, with a pencil in each hand. He was so bent over his work that his nose practically touched the page.

Lill cleared her throat. "We'd like to get a permit for a public show," she said. "It's an all-girl cowgirling wild west show. We're the Little Darlin's, and you ain't going to believe what we can do."

Mr. Stevens frowned. "Cowgirls you say? How many bucking broncs do you have?"

"We don't do bronc riding," said Rosey. "We do everything else."

He frowned. "I can sell you a permit," he said, "but no one will come. Not if you don't have bucking broncos."

"Wait a minute," said Lill. "We heard you have rodeo shows

here all the time. We heard people in this town like to see that sort of thing."

"True," he said. "We have a rodeo show every year. We just had one last month, in fact, with bucking-bronco riders. That's what people are used to seeing around here. If you don't have bronc riding, I'm afraid no-one's going to come and watch."

It was Lill that asked it. "Where do we get a horse that bucks?"

He smiled for the first time. "If you wanted the meanest most ornery critter you ever saw, go to the Parson place. Bloodshot's the wildest stallion ever born. A fellow went off him last month and broke his back in three places. He'll never walk again. If you get one of your little ladies to ride that thing, the whole town will be there."

"We'll take that permit anyway," Lill said as she slapped down two dollars.

When we got back to camp, she had us all gather around.

"We've got a chance to do something special here," she said. "We need to show this rodeo town that we're real rodeo stars. They've got a real rotten horse here, a crowd-draw bucking bronco so nasty he breaks people in half. Sorry, gals, but one of us has got to ride it."

Nobody spoke. No-one wanted to get picked.

"Only fair way," Lill said, "is the same way we pick our queens. It's time for a draw."

Rosey shook her head. "I ain't going to draw to get dead."

I said, "The last rider on Bloodshot didn't die. He just lost his back."

Rosey added, "And his walking."

Then Klara said Rosey *should* do it, since she had the strongest back.

But Rosey said Klara should do it, since she was good at staying on her cow.

Violet said Cilla should do it, since she was our trick rider.

Cilla said Glory that should do it, because she didn't do nothing else.

The arguing went back and forth a long time. Everyone had an idea about who should do it, as long as it wasn't herself.

But then Glory, who didn't ride at all, bowed her head. "Me," she said. "I'll do it. I'll ride that horse."

We all stared at her. She looked too serious to be joking.

"You can't," said Rosey. "You don't even know how to ride."

Glory shrugged. "I don't need to go anywhere. I just have to get on it. Isn't that right?"

"No," said Rosey. "You have to STAY on it."

But as hard as Rosey tried to talk her out of it, Glory stood firm. "I promised," she said, "to do what nobody else wanted to do. Now it's time."

I was worried for Glory, but at the same time, I felt a smidge of relief it wasn't going to be me on that horse. I'm sure I wasn't the only one who felt that way.

Lill considered it a while. Then she said, "All right. We'll do the show the same as always. But at the very end after Cilla's trick riding, we put Glory on the bronc. Glory, you don't have to stay on long. As soon as he's loose, you jump off right away, before that bad boy gets a chance to do too much damage. When you land, you act like you hurt your foot. You just look all pretty and painful. You won't need to get back in the saddle, they'll have seen what they came for. That's how we'll do it."

It was a good plan. A fine way to settle the matter. I helped wash up the plates and crawled into my blanket, not giving it any more concern.

But it wasn't settled. We didn't know it yet, but there was one of us who didn't agree with Lill's plan.

It wasn't until two days later that me and the rest of us found out.

INTERLUDE

- 28 -

Bloodshot was a black horse with a white mane. As striking as he was, it was his eyes that you noticed, even from a distance. They twisted and rolled around in his head in a way that told you everything you needed to know about this horse -- that you would be crazy to try to get on him.

It took the better part of the day just to chase him to the ring where we planned the show. You didn't lead this horse, you rounded him up like a bull, running from behind and cutting him off. It took all seven of us to do it and by the time we got him fenced it with the saddle strapped down, we were already shot.

The townspeople watched the whole process, just a few of them at first, then more as the morning went on. It was quite a crowd-pleaser just getting Bloodshot ready for the show, and those folks couldn't wait to see what else he'd do to us.

Once we started the show it was clear the people didn't care much about our acts. We rushed through the speed-riding and the shooting and the roping. We were too tired anyway to put much effort in.

It wasn't long before Cilla pranced around on Pal, waving her left hand in the air. She didn't even try for the double. Why bother with this crowd? Besides, Pal wasn't nearly as sure-footed as Dusty Blue. Heck, no horse on earth was as smart or as careful as him. I felt a surge of pride to know Dusty Blue was promised to me.

"Bring on the Bloodshot!" a voice yelled from the crowd. Then another voice chimed. Like wildfire the chant spread, until it had swelled to a whole chorus.

"We want Bloodshot! We want Bloodshot!" To me, it almost sounded like they were calling for blood*shed*.

Maybe they were.

I saw Glory head to the fence and my insides went cold. There was a hardness to her, a strange darkness to her face I could see even hid by the wig.

I ran to catch up with Rosey, Klara, and Lill, already there at his fence. I figured the four of us might be able to hold him back long enough for Glory's ride to look real.

Glory had other plans.

It was hard to hear much, with Bloodshot shorting and pawing the ground. But I heard Glory shout, "What are the rules?"

"Aint none," said Rosey. "The rider hangs un 'till he gets thrown."

"But their hands," Glory said. "Where do they put them?"

"One hangs onto the saddle horn," said Lill. "The other hand goes up in the air. That one can't touch the horse or the rider gets timed out."

"Which hand goes on the horn?" Glory asked.

"Does it matter?"

Glory bit her lip. Then she climbed up the fence posts above him.

"Don't hold the ropes," she said. "Once I'm on, just open the gate and get out the way."

This was not the plan. It was so unexpected I wasn't sure I'd heard her right.

"Now!" said Glory. Then she swung down from the fence and landed onto Bloodshot's back. Even before she had touched down, he went wild, his hind legs lashing out with enough power to kick us all to the moon.

"No!" cried Rosey. "You can't ride him for real!"

Lill, already at the gate, pushed it wide open. Bloodshot rocketed out, heaving and buckling to throw Glory off. With her left arm held high, she twisted forward and backwards so hard I thought her back would snap.

He bounced and bucked for all he was worth, but somehow she stayed on. As I watched, the rest of the world seemed to fall away, like the whole world was spinning around that one crazy horse and the mad woman atop him. He kicked so high there were times I swear could see blue sky and clouds between her body and the saddle. But her rump managed to land back on it, like she was tied to it somehow.

Then I saw why. She'd wrapped the reins around her saddle-horn hand. I shivered inside. Her arms were long and thin like fancy table legs – they were surely not meant to take such abuse.

I heard the crack before I saw her arm go funny and bend the wrong way. Even then, it took another few kicks and contortions before Bloodshot could rid himself of her. I saw Glory's body sail up above him in a slow summersault -- head over feet, feet over head -- until she landed, with an even louder crack, on her back in the dirt.

Lill, always the fastest, got to her first, with Rosey not far behind.

"Why?" Rosey cried. "Why?"

Glory's eyes fluttered as she looked up at us. "Did I do it? Did I beat the town record?"

Lill said, "Only if you stay with us, bronc rider. It don't count if you die."

Trust Lill to say the one thing to make Glory try to hang on.

Glory smiled, a faint little twinge on her lips before her eyes rolled into the back of her head.

*

We hauled Glory to the local doc's office. He said she was

alive, but just barely. We laid her out on a soft pad of pillows where he could watch her. He told us a coma was a good thing, because that meant she wasn't feeling the pain. She laid stretched out cold for three days, but finally woke up, with her arm broken and bruises everywhere else. We took turns sitting with her, with the doc watching over the whole time. He'd seen her yellow hair – the only man in town who had -- and he seemed kind of sweet on her.

I think most of the town was sweet on her, because they treated us like heroes just for knowing her.

We couldn't leave town without her, not after what she'd done for us. The villagers put us up, like we were celebrities, too. Rosey and I were lodged with an older couple in the center of town. Violet and Klara went to a log house with a big family full of kids, while they put Cilla and Lill in a room at the back of the church.

It was fine at first. We all had regular meals and were never asked to lift a finger for anything.

But after a while it grew stale. We'd been on the open road so long it was hard to live in a box with strangers, even kind ones.

Most of all, I missed not having the others around. I would notice something and turn to tell Violet or Lill, but I would have to stop myself because they weren't there. I missed life under the stars. I missed Dusty Blue who was tied up behind the church with Cilla. And after a while, I even missed the bickering.

It was a week before Glory could sit up, and another week before she could do it without pain. But then, with Rosey holding her up, we brought her to the little room at the back of the church with all seven of us squeezed into that space. Violet passed around pieces of a *welcome back* pie. It had a berry filling, hot and tart with a velvety-buttery crust. I think that pie was one of Violet's best ever, and that was saying a lot.

With her arm in a cast, Glory sat amongst us, her dish balanced on her lap.

"I can cut your pie into little tiny pieces for you," said Lill, "since your good hand's laid up."

Glory smiled. "No need. I'm left-handed. I'll eat in a moment. For now, I'm just enjoying being back."

Rosey frowned. "Left-handed? They why did you hang on with your right?"

Glory shrugged. "I knew whatever hand I hung on with, that's what I'd break. So I gave it my bad arm. That way if it busted off, I wouldn't lose anything I really needed."

I couldn't believe she had planned the whole thing, knowing her arm would suffer terrible pain. I couldn't imagine how she went through with it. It was her bones that broke; her will never quit.

I had come to realize many things about the Darlin's. We were all strong-minded souls. In my own quiet way, I was as stubborn as the rest. We put up with hardships and danger, and let nothing get in our way.

But for what she had done, for the way she hung onto that horse even after her bones had cracked, Glory was the bravest of us all.

Someone laughed and we all joined in. It felt so good to be all back together.

"What do you say we blow this town?" said Lill. "I'm sick of being cooped up here. Who's ready to get back to the open road?"

I felt the same way. Rosey and Klara did, too. And Violet – too busy feeding her host family's children for man hunting – agreed. But it wasn't all up to us. There was only one person's agreement that mattered.

We all turned to Glory.

"I'm ready."

We cheered. The Darlin's were back in business, and didn't we know it.

We congratulated ourselves and gorged our stomachs on

Violet's pie. That's when Klara drifted to the window.

I saw her tap gently on the glass.

"Look," she said.

We huddled around and saw what she saw. Blowing down from above there were tiny white flakes from the heavens. The first hint of snow.

Our carefree cowgirling summer was about to end.

THE PRICE TO PAY

- 29 -

Lill laid out the map she picked up in Soda Springs and we gathered around it. Lill said, "With winter breathing down our necks, we have just enough time to get to one place, if we push it and don't stop to do shows."

"How far to the Pacific Coast?" Violet asked.

Cilla said, "It's only one state away."

"Yes," Lill added. "But that state's a big one. We'd have to go through the whole length of Oregon."

"It would be a hard push," said Rosey. "Through a mountain range and all."

Cilla leaned over the map. "The Blue Mountains? That can't be a big range, can it? Who's even heard of them?"

Rosey frowned. "Before we got lost in it, I never heard of the Bridger Forest, either."

Cilla scowled. For someone who argued all the time, she didn't like being challenged.

"We can't keep heading west," said Rosey. "Just think of the Donner party."

"What kind of party?" Klara asked.

Rosey frowned. "The kind where a hundred people take off through the hills, get caught in the winter, and got nothing to eat but each other."

Once she'd said it, I recalled Mama telling me a story like that. I thought it was a tale to coax little girls into behaving. I never knew it was real.

Lill said, "It's time to go east, to Denver."

"Through the Rockies?" said Violet.

"This is a sign," Lill said. "Don't you see? Buffalo Bill's not in Cody, but we've got just enough time to get to him in Denver before winter really sets in. The plan was always to join him. We've done all right on our own, and polished our acts. Now it's time to show him what we can do. Once he sees, he'll take us for sure! We can winter with him and practice new acts. Oh, I can't wait to meet him. I've wanted this for so long!"

Cilla said, "I think we should go south. My family has a uranium mining camp in Moab. That's in Utah, the southern part of the state. It's warm there in the winter. We can hold up there until spring. After that we can go chasing after Buffalo Bill."

"Your family owns a mine?" Rosey asked. "I don't believe it for a second. If you came from landed folks, why the heck would you be tromping around with us?"

"My family is rich," said Cilla. "So I will be, too, someday. What I do in the meantime is my own business."

Rosey snorted.

"Uranium?" said Vi. "Isn't that dangerous?"

"Only if it's there," said Cilla. "They dug it all out. That's why the mining camp's been abandoned. It's empty, just waiting for us."

"I don't care where we go," said Glory. "As long as it's far from Helena." That was the first time Glory let it slip where she was from.

"In Montana?" said Cilla. "That's way up north. The farthest direction from there would be south. Glory, we really should go south."

"Sounds good to me," Glory said.

"You would be safer in the east," Lill said. "We'd all be safe with Buffalo Bill. Heck, we're so good now we could probably headline his show. We'd be famous for sure. We have to get to him. We just have to."

Rosey said, "It makes more sense to wait until after winter's through."

"It can't wait," said Lill. "I feel it in my bones. As clear as I know my own name, I *know* that if we don't find him soon, it will be too late. This is our chance. This is our time to shine."

We all looked at Lill. We couldn't help it. We'd seen her excited before, but now that girl was glowing like a sunrise and fireworks all rolled up together.

"All right," said Glory, "East to Denver."

"Too late," said Cilla. "You've already voted south. You can't change once you've voted. So that's two votes for the south, Glory and me, and Lill's got one vote in for the east. Violet?"

Violet looked at Cilla, then at Lill. Both of them wanted her vote. I knew Violet didn't want to vote against Lill. But something else was holding her back. Finally Violet said, "The last time I gambled everything on a man I never met, it didn't turn out so well. But whatever you all pick, that will be fine with me."

"Myself as well," said Klara, excusing herself from the vote, too.

That left only Rosey and me.

I caught Rosey's eye. I could almost hear her thoughts. She figured I'd vote against Cilla like I always did. Rosey thought we had the vote all sewed up.

She said, "Cilla might have thought up the show, but cowgirling was in Lill's head right from the first. I'm voting with Lill on this one. I say we go east."

Rosey leaned up against the wall and folded her arms over her chest as if the matter was all set.

But it wasn't. There was still me. My vote was the swing vote, the one that would determine our fate.

Cilla looked at me and smiled. Like a wolf.

The skin on my back felt all prickly and cold. This was the biggest choice we'd ever made. If I voted against Lill, it would break her heart.

My voice went dry inside me. Everyone stared at me.

"Maisy?" said Lill, "are you all right?"

"Maybe she needs some tonic," said Cilla, her sharp little eyes boring into me. "I saw a doctor make a tonic one time. From ground-up horse meat. It was an old horse nobody wanted anymore, so they whacked it dead and gutted the parts."

I didn't like Cilla, but I had never actually hated her before.

"Come on, Maisy," Rosey said. "Give us the word."

It was a horrible choice. Lill's dream or Dusty Blue's life.

"South," I mumbled.

Rosey shook her head as if she couldn't believe it. "What did you say?"

"You heard me," I told her. "I said south. Now leave me alone."

Rosey stumbled back into the wall as if she'd been hit.

Lill turned away. She didn't want us to see her eyes watering up.

But I could feel it. We all could. I had betrayed her.

Cilla smiled so hard I thought she'd grin her face off. I don't know how her lips could hold that pose for so long, but she gloated for what seemed like days.

*

Cilla told us it was only 200 miles to Moab. But like a lot of things Cilla said, that wasn't true.

We packed up the next morning and headed out, but we didn't go south at first. We backtracked along the Snake River valley, all the way to Burley before we peeled off to the south.

Glory was livid about that. She did not want to go back through those same Idaho towns we had just came from. Especially not Buhl where everyone at the show had seen her without the wig.

But it had the best roads, so we didn't have much choice. We didn't stop anywhere very long. We rode all day, every day, until we couldn't ride anymore. When we stopped, we barely touched down for the night and were off again in the morning.

From Delco we headed south into Utah, skirting the North Salt Flats with its great swarms of migrating geese. Then we dropped into the Salt Lake basin, a big flat dish of a valley with misty mountains along the far sides.

It was early November by now, late 1916, and we were not the only ones chased by a cold wind. Europe broke out in war. America was not in it yet and trying its hardest to stay out. But that war was like a black fire, eating everything in its path. There was no way to stop it. No way to keep it from sucking more and more countries in. We tried to ignore it, but it was like a shadow that wouldn't go away.

That year was an election year, and the war turned the presidential election into a spectacle, the biggest show around. First, they thought President Wilson won his second term. Then they announced that it was Hughes who had won. But later, they said they made a mistake and that it was Wilson with the most votes after all. It took days to figure out what happened and who was in charge.

None of us voted. We were too busy putting miles behind us. On and on we rode, through the spine of the state -- American Fork, Orem, Provo. From there we cut southeast to Price, then down to Green River.

Finally, with the whole country holding its breath, hoping against hope that Wilson could keep us out of war, we made it to Moab.

But besides the war brewing, there was another black cloud churning on the horizon. This one was smaller, but the grudge it bore was personal. As the whole country lay tipped to lose its innocence, we were about to lose much more.

THE STRANGER

- 30 -

A pale man in a black coat rode into Bozeman, Montana, wiping a swath of sweat from his face. He tied up his horse outside a saloon and headed for the bar, looking right, then left, then right again. Inside he saw three woozy drunks at the counter slumped over their drinks, their beer mugs drained of even the foam. They smelled like sour milk and donkey piss. He wondered how many more bars like this he would have to endure.

Whatever the cost, he knew he'd pay it. Nothing was more important than completing his task.

"Bartender," he called out. "Buy a drink for these three fine gentlemen. It's on me."

That got their attention. The drunks turned to assess their benefactor. He was tall and grim in his long city coat, the refined clothes of a well-to-to business man. But his pants were worn shiny from long hours spent in the saddle.

"Thank you kindly," said the drunk in the red shirt. "A friend in deed is a friend for me." He laughed at his own joke so hard he began to choke. The man in the coat looked on, his eyes betraying no emotion at all.

The bartender, a portly man with suspenders that stained against his belly re-filled their mugs. The two other men tipped their heads at the stranger. He drank nothing himself but waited for them to finish. He was a patient man.

When the mugs had been drained dry, the man in the black coat reached into a pocket and withdrew a packet. In it was a photograph of a girl. A tattered black and white photograph with a tear down one side. Even so, it was clear that the girl was pretty, with straw-colored hair.

The stranger cleared his throat. "I'm wondering if any of you gentlemen have seen this girl." He passed the photograph down.

"Hair like an angel," said the drunk in the checkered shirt. "Can't say that I have."

The stranger nodded. "What about you?"

The other two shook their heads.

The photograph was slid back down the bar, then slipped back into his black coat pocket. The stranger stood up, preparing to leave.

"Wait a minute," said the drunk in the suede vest. "I heard a story from a fellow I used to ride with. He saw a girl once, with hair you didn't forget, as bright as the sun. He just saw her for a second, in a rodeo show. But just that one glimpse stole his heart."

Suede vest paused as if he had more to tell, for the right inducement.

"Bartender," said the long coat stranger. "Another round for my friends."

With the mugs re-filled, suede-vest continued his story. "My friend fell so hard for this beauty that he give her a horse. A good-looking horse, since she was a real looker. She took his horse but didn't give him two kind words, not even a thanks. Maybe she's your goldy girl."

"A rodeo show?" said the man in the black coat. "When? Where did this happen?"

"Don't know nothing more about it. I ain't seen him in days. It was his story, not mine."

Checkered shirt piped up. "I saw a rodeo show a while back. It was all girls in it. There weren't no blondey-girls, I'd have remembered that. But some weren't too bad looking."

"I heard tell of them. Yeah, supposed to be pretty good. Though I never saw them myself."

"What else can you tell me?" asked the man in the long coat.

They all went quiet. Suede vest looked into his empty mug.

"Bartender," said the man in the black coat. "Can we have another round here?"

"You can buy me another drink," said red shirt. "But I can't tell you nothing else, because that's all I know." The other two mumbled in agreement.

The man in the black coat nodded to himself. "Honest men. I like that. Bartender, another round for these good men all the same. Then I'll settle my bill and be on my way."

The bartender wiped his hands on his pants, then topped up the three mugs one more time. He gave the stranger his bill. The stranger paid it, tipped his hat, then headed for the door.

"Wait a minute," said checkered shirt. "Last I heard, I think they was heading south. They was called the Little Dreamers, or something like that."

For the first time since he'd come in, the stranger's lips twitched sideways. It was not much to go on, but it was more than he came in with.

Maybe, just maybe, it would be enough.

CILLA'S MINE

- 31 -

It was just after dark when we pulled into Moab, and we were bone tired. We'd come a long way, much farther than we expected. At least Cilla was right about one thing. The climate was warmer here. Not tropical by any means, or even balmy. But the sun was brighter here than everywhere else we'd been, and the mud lining the creek beds was wet, without even a trace of ice.

Cilla's mining camp was still five miles past town, but we were too tired to push on. We chose to rest for the night. We paid a farmer to rent us his bunkhouse and barn for the evening, then went into town for a meal. Violet was too tired to cook. Besides, Moab would be our supply town for the winter and it wouldn't hurt to see what was there.

We had a fine stew at the hotel cafe, with beef chunks and potatoes, our backs warmed by a roaring fire. We were all in good spirits, even Glory in her wig-hat that she always wore in town.

The landlady for the hotel, Mrs. Kestling, was also the cook. To help pay for our meal, Violet offered to help out in the kitchen. Before dinner was over, Mrs. Kestling was mighty impressed with Violet's cooking. She put in a standing order to buy three pies from Violet every week. So it was Violet who got the first job in town, without hardly even trying.

That night while the others were settled into their bunks, I went out to find Dusty Blue in his stall. I patted his neck, smoothing the smoky gray threads of his mane. He liked when I did that.

"You can't slip your halter anymore," I said, stroking his halter so he'd understand what I was talking about. "Once we get to Cilla's mining camp, we're supposed to live like everybody else, with me indoors with the people and you in a stall like this."

I think he understood because he looked kind of sad.

"But I'll still take you out," I said. "It's just that I'll have to come and get you. Not the other way around."

To show what I meant, I opened the gate to his stall and he followed me out. There was a little hill on the north side of town and we climbed it until Moab spread below us like a dark jewel, punctuated by pinpoints of light. I could see the hotel and Mrs. Kestling's house behind it. There was a clothesline out back, empty now. It reminded me I had not yet asked about mending.

A tidy row of houses stretched off to the right, dotted by shops. Towards the far edge, I could see the cross of a church. No doubt that's where Violet would attend. Just opposite it on the other side of the street was a saloon. A rowdy place, by the noise of it, and the rinky-tink piano tune carried all the way to me. It would take some work to keep Rosey away from that place.

There it was, a perfect little gem of a town. Now it was our town.

Somewhere, out there in the red rock, five miles to the south, was Cilla's mining camp. Our winter home. I couldn't see it yet but I knew it was there, just waiting for us.

*

The next morning we had a pancake breakfast and rode off, eager to see our winter home. We asked Cilla a hundred questions about the camp, but she wouldn't answer a single one. She said she wanted it to be a surprise.

We got there mid-morning with the sun a white ball in the early winter sky. The mining camp was right where the map said it was -- *The Mother Lode Mine*. But as we rounded the turn and got our first sight, we froze like statues. Even Cilla.

The place was a dump.

A handful of shacks scattered around. Some had already fallen down, and the rest were well on their way. The stable, out back, had no roof. There was broken glass and spiked shreds of mining gear everywhere. We couldn't bring the horses in close without cutting their legs.

Rosey picked her way over the rubble mounds to the outhouse. As soon as she touched it, it toppled to its side and splintered .

Cilla started to squawk. "You broke it. How dare you! Fix it, Rosey. Fix it *right now*."

At that moment, I thought about the Donner party. I knew who I'd eat first.

Then Glory spoke up. "This isn't so bad. We take wood from the shacks that fell down and shore up the good ones. We rake the garbage into a ring and plant a garden inside. It won't bloom yet, but we'll have flowers and vegetables next spring."

The more Glory talked, the more I could see what she had in mind.

So we stayed. With winter nipping at our heels, we didn't have much choice.

The first thing we fixed was the barn. The horses needed to be out of the wind. Those first nights, we slept in there with them, all of us huddled together for warmth.

Little by little, with scavenged wood, we fixed up a cabin. I wove a rug out of weeds. Rosey built a new door to replace the one that was missing. Klara cleaned the mouse-littered floor with pine boughs, and Lill found a barrel for a stove. When Violet cooked our first meal on that wood stove, it smelled smoky and good. It almost looked like a home.

For the first few days, we all slept in that little cabin on the floor. As we fixed the camp up, we began to spread out.

Some days we made a little progress, some days we made

more. We went into town to take on odd jobs here and there to pay for supplies. There was so much to do, that first month we were always dead tired when the sun went down.

It was a constant battle to keep the stove fire going, and not easy finding enough weed grass to feed our horses, but we managed.

We had no time to cowgirl with our lives consumed by domestic chores. But our labor kept us limber and strong.

Except Cilla. She said her ownership gave her immunity from helping out. We couldn't argue that out of her. On those times she did lend a hand, her complaining was worse than her help. She wound up drifting off into town as she pleased, never to take on jobs or do anything useful. I didn't know what she did in town all day, and I didn't care.

I probably should have. Ignoring Cilla was always a mistake.

HUNKERING DOWN FOR WINTER

- 32 -

After a while, it felt good having our own place. I got used to the routine, and knew every morning when I woke up exactly where I was. I went into town every few days, sometimes with Violet to get staples or deliver her pies. Klara took on some washing, and I mended all kinds of things.

Rosey picked up jobs shoeing horses. I always went with her, mostly to help. But also to keep my eye on her, to make sure she didn't nip into the bar.

Pretty soon between our odd jobs, we were taking in almost as much as we did from the shows.

Lill took care of the money. That was her job. She collected what people owed us, kept track of it all, and paid our bills at the store. She was better than a bank. If we needed something, all we had to do was clear it with Lill.

One time I wanted muslin to make pillows.

She thought about it a minute, then said. "We can afford three yards. Go pick it up whenever you want. If you need more, ask me next week."

That's how it was. I didn't have to carry money around. The amounts were all in Lill's head. She had a real mind for numbers. She said it was easy, just a trick she learned tending bar back in Jackson Hole.

I think Lill was a lot smarter than she ever let on.

I liked that town. The people were friendly enough. It did take some getting used to the fact that they knew more about me than I knew of them. But I wasn't too worried about Cilla's loose lips anymore. By this time, I had turned 16 and was of age in every state.

Violet didn't like it, though. She didn't like all the men-folk hearing about her from Cilla before she could meet them herself. Cilla made her sound like a gun-slinger. That wasn't the real Violet at all.

One time Vi came back from town madder than a whole nest of wasps. She marched up to Cilla and just let her have it, right in front of us all.

"How dare you," said Violet. "Why did you tell all those people I sleep with my gun? You're scaring my suitors away. Lill, make her stop talking about me!"

Lill shrugged. "But you do sleep with your gun. She's not spreading lies. You want me to put a lock on her mouth? I can't. As long as she's not talking about Glory, I can't tell her what to say any more than I could plug up the wind."

Violet was not pleased.

"We're here," Lill told Violet, "because you wouldn't vote with me. So don't be complaining if you don't like the way it's turned out."

Violet stomped off, and wound up at the courthouse in Moab. Pouring over the records, she made a list of every male in town. She worked on her list for days, making notes -- how old, what they did, what they owned -- until it was practically a book. The book of male prospects.

Armed with these pages, she proceeded down the list to meet them, going through every single unmarried male who still had some teeth.

Mostly she met them at church. But despite all her efforts, the search for Mr. Right was turning out wrong. More often than not, she would return from town in a snit. Then Rosey would say, "Your list is getting shorter every day."

I didn't tell Rosey to her face, but I thought she was being mean. This was Violet's dream, and a person's dream is precious.

I should know. I had stabbed Lill's dream through the heart.

Lill still woke up early every morning to ride Thunder. I saw them sometimes when I took out Dusty Blue.

One crisp morning, as Lill and Thunder came back from their ride, Lill's cheeks flushed from the wind, I was there waiting for them in the barn.

"I'm guessing you want to talk to me about something," said Lill as she slid down from Thunder to brush him down.

I nodded, unsure how to begin. "You know I've been doing mending for Mrs. Kestling and her friends. I know I need to pay for my share of the food. But..." After that, my words failed me. I didn't know how to explain it so I wouldn't sound greedy.

Lill said, "You want to know if you can keep part of your cut? To save it up for something big? As big as a horse?"

I couldn't believe that she knew.

She said, "You don't say much in words, Maisy Daisy, but your eyes give you away. I see how you look at that gray horse. I know what it's like to get up before everyone else, just to get that one little part of the day when you don't share him with anyone else. Of course I know that. How could I miss it?"

Did that mean that she also knew...

"I was upset for a while," she went on. "But I figured that's why you voted to come here. That day that we voted, I remember Cilla talking about killing a horse. I know you were scared for Dusty Blue."

I was stunned. She'd figured out what I'd done and was still talking to me.

"I see I was right," she said. "I know Cilla can be... difficult. I'm not blind to her bad side, no matter what Rosey thinks. I know Cilla gets it wrong, some times. Maybe most times. But she does it for the right reasons. She does it for the group. The Darlin's was her idea after all, and we owe her for that."

That part was true. But I still didn't trust Cilla's motives.

"I'll tell you what," said Lill. "From now on, when I collect your pay from Mrs. Kestling and her pals, I'll put half into the kitty and half into a separate account that's just for you. You earn more than your share anyway, so it makes sense you should keep some for yourself. In fact, I'll go ahead and move half of what you've made since we've been here from the general fund into your personal fund. Once I do that, you'll have..." and here she stopped to do the adding in her head. "...twenty dollars towards Dusty Blue. How much do you need?"

"Two hundred and fifty dollars," I said.

She whistled. "That will take a while, but don't worry, Maisy. You'll get there. Sooner or later you'll buy that gray horse."

I was so overwhelmed I almost dropped to my knees. "Thank you," I said. The words sounded flat in my ears. I wanted to say something grander. She deserved so much more than that but I didn't know how to say it.

"Don't mention it," she said with a smile. Then she went back to brushing Thunder's withers. "Just one thing," she added. "Do you ever play cards?"

"Not much."

"Good," she said. "No matter what Rosey might tell you, stay away from poker. With your face, you'd be slaughtered."

DUSTUP

- 33 -

While we were in town, Glory kept busy, too, planning her garden. It was too early to plant, but not too early to dig. Glory cornered off a courtyard with posts and some rope, and dug in little trenches that went back and forth, up and down, showing exactly where the rows of plants would go. It was quite an elaborate plan she had mapped out, with early spring flowers planned for the front rows, with later spring flowers behind them and summer bloomers in the back. That way, she said, we'd have constant garden. A perpetual explosion of buds. And right in the center of it all, with a little path that led through all the rest, was a circle of all of the blossoms on our moose hide crown.

Cilla didn't appreciate Glory's plans. She frowned at Glory whenever she walked by. Glory didn't seem to notice. She just hummed away as she turned over the soil with a trowel, prepping it, she said, to make it soft and nutritious for when it was time to plant.

For a while, Cilla kept her disapproval to herself. But Cilla being Cilla, I knew she'd let it out sooner or later.

We were all in the cook shack, all seven of us, and had just finished supper. Klara and I were cleaning the plates. There was a lot to clean up that night because it was one of Vi's more daring recipes, pumpkin casserole with mint leaves. It was not a good combination. Vi was not pleased to see how much didn't get eaten, and we were still hungry so no one was in a good mood to start with.

Right in the middle of all that, Cilla turned to Glory and said, "I don't think you should have a garden."

"Why not?" said Glory. "The climate's perfect."

Cilla shook her head. "That's not what I mean. What I'm saying is that I don't like the idea. It's not your camp, you know. You don't own it. It's one thing to fix up the cabins, but why do you have to re-arrange everything, even the dirt?"

"What's the problem with that?" said Rosey. "She's making it better. She's working hard. That's more than I could say for you. You don't do anything around here. Or for the show."

"You know very well what I do for the Darlin's," said Cilla. "Without me, no one would ever show up to see us. Don't you remember Twin Falls? The show where nobody came?"

Rosey growled. "Maybe nobody came because they knew you'd be there. Maybe they heard of a rider who's only trick was that she had no tricks, so they all stayed away."

"Or maybe," said Cilla, "they stayed away because they heard there was a bull-dogger so ugly she could scare a bull into submission, just by showing her face."

Rosey stood up so fast that her stool tipped over.

Cilla stood up, too, but with Rosey towering over her like a bear, Cilla realized that was a mistake. Her eyes went wild looking for Lill, the only one of us who could back Rosey down.

Lill popped up between them like a rabbit. "That's enough," she said. "Sit down right now."

Rosey did not sit. "I'm tired of the way Cilla always picks on Glory. She's been against Glory from the start. I'd have thought Cilla would be glad to have someone who did less in the show. Somebody who made her stupid flag tricks look good. But no, she has to chew away at Glory every chance she gets. Even after Glory rode that horse. Why, Glory showed more talent in that one ride than Cilla's shown all season."

"Talent?" said Cilla. "That wasn't talent, that was stupidity. And if I have to hear about Glory's ride one more time, I'm going to be sick. Glory, Glory, Glory. Everybody always talking about Glory, breaking her arm. But what about me? I rode Glory's horse in that same show. How was I supposed to know Pal wasn't as safe as Dusty Blue? Didn't you all see how nervous he was in that show? Good thing I didn't do double flag hands at Nampa. If I had, I could have been killed. But does anyone appreciate the risk I took? No, indeed. It's always about Glory, and never about me."

"It was Glory in danger, not you," said Rosey. "The only danger you were in was in looking like a fool."

"Stop that right now, both of you," said Lill. "Is that what this is about? What *didn't* happen in Nampa? Well then, your lives must be pretty darn grand if all you have to complain about is something that didn't happen."

Rosey sat down, her forehead scrunched up in thought. And once again, Lill had said the exact right thing to deal with the situation.

But while that fight was diffused, the underlying tension beneath it was still there. As long as Cilla was Cilla, she was bound to set Rosey off again. And there was no guarantee Lill would be there the next time around.

There was something else that bothered me about that whole exchange. Cilla said Pal was Glory's horse. But didn't the man give it to Cilla in the end? If it wasn't Cilla's horse, whose was it? And if Cilla couldn't ride Pal in the show, she was not going to want to sell Dusty Blue.

But then, I realized, that wouldn't affect me. I already had her word she would sell him. We agreed. It didn't matter that we made that deal before the Nampa show. A promise was a promise. Cilla couldn't take it back now.

I had been thinking that I'd been too hasty to agree to Cilla's terms. Maybe I'd been too quick about the whole thing. Maybe if I waited, I wouldn't have had to sell off my vote. And if I'd waited for Dusty Blue to get older, the asking price could have been much less.

But as I took in more and more mending, my account grew every day. By the time spring rolled around, I knew I might just have enough. That thought was the fire that kept me going, and fueled my hopeful dreams.

*

One day, after Cilla had gone into town with Lill, I was sitting on my bunk putting patches on a pair of dark blue pants. All of a sudden I saw something flash by the window. It was Klara, arms outstretched, her dark hair streaming behind her. She was so high up it looked like she was flying.

I ran to the door.

I saw right away that she wasn't flying. She was on the back of Dusty Blue, standing straight up, her bare feet on the leather of his saddle, hanging on in a pigeon-toed grip. He was galloping around in a circle by Glory's garden patch. But the crazy thing was that Klara didn't look shaky up there, she looked happy and free.

I couldn't believe it. I knew Klara had good balance with riding her cow but I didn't know she could stand on top of a racing horse.

I wondered how long she'd been practicing. How long she'd been sneaking Dusty Blue out of his stall right under Cilla's nose.

I felt jealous.

Then I saw Rosey, grinning – but not surprised.

"Stop," Klara commanded. Obediently, Dusty Blue stopped in his tracks. Klara dropped down into the saddle, flipping her leg sideways. Then she slid off, like it was the easiest thing in the world.

"How long has she been doing this trick?" I asked Rosey.

"About a week."

Klara led Dusty Blue over to us. Rosey took his reins. "I'll bring him in," said Rosey, leading the gray horse away.

Klara smiled, pleased with herself.

I shook my head in wonder. "So, now we'll have two trick riders in the show, eh?"

Klara frowned. "I won't do that in the show. Cilla is our trick rider. I only ride the cow."

"But you're so good up there," I said. "Why wouldn't you want to show off what you can do?"

"You've seen how hard Cilla is on Glory," said Klara. "Ever since Glory rode the bronc, Cilla has been jealous. Just think how she would treat me if she knew I could do that."

"You don't have to tip-toe around Cilla," I said. "This isn't her show. She's not..."

Suddenly I heard a sound that jolted through me. A horse's call of distress. From Dusty Blue.

I snapped my head around to see.

Rosey had balanced a pail of water on top of Dusty Blue's saddle and was making him trot. It was a choppy pace, and with every step, the water was splishing and sploshing over the sides.

For some horses, it would not have been such a problem. But he was not like most horses. He knew it was his job to protect his cargo, whether it was a human or something the human needed. It was a responsibility he did not take lightly, and with the water splashing out, he was failing his task. He was letting his humans down, and when a horse is upset, it goes right through his brain and turns into panic.

Rosey was taunting him, making it worse. "Priscilla Pystunia, our little Miss Prissy Pissy, thinks she's so smart because she can ride this horse. But that's no trick. Anybody can ride this thing. Even a bucket of ice."

The poor horse was completely beside himself by now, sure he had harmed his burden – sure he had done something terribly wrong.

I ran to him, and just as I got there, the bucket tipped over and cold water hit us both like a wall.

He screamed in fear and reared up. I jumped in front of him. Normally, you wouldn't do that with a horse -- you'd get trampled. But Dusty Blue wasn't just any horse. I knew that even in a panic he would not drop his legs on me.

"Steady, boy," I said catching his harness and easing him down. "Not your fault. None of this is your fault. Good boy, Dusty Blue. Don't worry. You didn't break anything. It was only water. Everything's all right."

I looked over at Rosey, laughing so hard she was holding her sides. I was so angry it felt like a rock had grown in my chest.

"You take Dusty Blue," I told Klara. "Get him in the barn and dry him off. I have words for Rosey that this horse doesn't need to hear. He's already been upset enough for one day."

Klara led Dusty Blue away and Rosey stopped laughing. She could tell I was mad.

"I was only having a little fun."

"Fun?" I exploded. "You call that fun? What kind of cheap stunt is that, to make fun of that horse? He already has to deal with Cilla. That's bad enough. But even Cilla doesn't treat him like that. He's never done anything to you. All he's done is protect you. And all of us. You might think you're better than Cilla, but I've never seen her do anything that low. It makes me sick to even think of it. And I thought you were a friend."

My words hit Rosey hard, as much as if I had punched her.

I was glad. I wanted her to hurt.

I ran into the bunkhouse and threw my mending on the floor. Then I hurled myself onto my bed and pulled my blanket over me.

I stayed there, curled up in a ball. Maybe crying, maybe not. I don't remember. All I know is that no one came near me. They all knew to stay away.

I didn't crawl out from that blanket for a very long time.

*

After that, I avoided Rosey, and she stayed away from me. We were hardly even in the same room together. This wasn't easy in the cramped quarters of the camp, but we managed.

Then Rosey moved out of the bunkhouse. I don't know where she went. Maybe she put up a cot in the wood shed. Or maybe she slept under the wagon.

Wherever it was, I didn't care. If that was how she was going to be, it was her choice. I had sewing to do anyway, and I threw myself into that.

Lill tried to talk to me, but I wouldn't have it. I didn't want to hear it. Rosey was wrong, that's all there was to it.

The others didn't say anything about it. They pretended not to notice. Like it never happened.

But of course it did.

A couple of days went by, and sometimes my anger felt like a disease that eats you up from the inside. Sometimes it was hard to stay mad.

But then I'd think of it, about the fear in Dusty Blue's eyes and how Rosey never even said she was sorry, and I'd get mad all over again.

The days went by, each one as gray as the last. Klara and Violet went into town and brought me sewing to mend, and that's all I did. I didn't go into town myself. I didn't even ride Dusty Blue. I just stayed in the bunkhouse and patched frocks and sewed hook and eyes. When I was done with the mending, I made things. Thick blankets and sweaters and hook rugs, in every type of yarn or cloth scraps that Klara could get her hands on for me.

When I was done with a piece, Klara would take what I made and sell it in town. I didn't ask how much she got for it. For any of it. I didn't need to know. Lill would keep track. Lill would remember.

But I didn't ask Lill. Because then Lill would want to talk about other things, and I knew what she'd say. That I was being pig-headed. And maybe I was.

But Rosey was wrong. And nothing Lill could say, or anyone else, was going to change that.

STALEMATE

- 34 -

The gray days stretched on, and the black nights grew longer. Before I knew it, the Christmas season was upon us.

Klara brought me requests -- people wanting long stockings to hang on their fireplace in red and white yarns. I made plenty of those, with children's names stitched in big letters across the top.

We'd been at the camp for over six weeks and this was our first big holiday celebration at the Mother Lode, not counting Thanksgiving which somehow slipped by us. Maybe that's why Violet became so obsessed with the Christmas dinner. On Christmas Eve she locked herself inside the cook shack and wouldn't let us in. Not even Klara. We drifted around camp and wherever we went -- to the bunkhouse or the woodshed or outhouse -- we could hear Glory singing her Christmas songs, her voice as high and sweet as a flute.

Singing was what Glory was made for. Too bad it wasn't a rodeo sport.

When Violet finally let us in the cook shack, we found the table spilling over with food. There was so much it hurt my stomach just to look at it all, but that didn't stop me from digging in.

I had just finished my first plate of turkey and biscuits when Lill came in -- I didn't even notice she'd been gone. She said, "I think Dusty Blue has a pebble in his hoof. He seems to be favoring one side."

I ran out to the stables -- didn't even stop to put on my Father's barn coat -- and raced to Dusty Blue's stall.

He wasn't there. None of the horses were there. Only Rosey, her face pasty white, drained of color.

"Is he all right?" I asked, fearing the worse.

"Here," she said, handing me a bag. "Open it up. It's something you need."

I was afraid to look. What could it be? His death certificate? His bloody brand mark sliced off, like she'd done with old Prize? Or was it a pebble that got stuck in his foot and gave him gangrene or...

She opened the bag. It was full of money. Not just coins, it was stuffed with bills.

"It's for you," she said. "One hundred and eighty dollars. With the money Lill's holding for you, it's just about enough to buy your horse."

I didn't understand.

"After you got so upset," Rosey continued, "Glory said I should talk to Lill. She said Lill could tell me all about it. I didn't know Dusty Blue was special to you. I just thought since he was Cilla's... well, I just didn't know. I was wrong."

"You talked to Lill? She told you everything? And Glory knew, too? How?"

Rosey shrugged. "Maisy, look how we live. There's no room for secrets between us. I should have known Dusty Blue was different. I was just plain stupid. I'm sorry. I've been wanting to tell you that for a long time now. But it just seemed like useless words, until I could back it up with something more powerful. Here is that something."

"You've... been sorry all this time?"

She nodded.

"Where's this money from?"

"I went into town," she said. "It was easy, without you shadowing me around. Last night I had one little drink, that led to another, and the next thing I knew, I won the whole pot! Lill snatched it up before I could lose it back. Can you believe it? For once in my life, I came out ahead. I want you to have it. You deserve that horse. And he deserves you."

I was so stunned I could hardly talk. "He's not sick? He's alive?"

Rosey laughed. "He's fine. He's out back with the others, eating a special carrot and oat cake Violet baked for them. With molasses frosting. Can you believe it?"

I didn't know what to say.

"You had every right to be mad at me," she said. "I'd have felt the same if someone did that to Big Red."

"Rosey, I can't take your money."

"You have to," she said. "Because if you give it back to me, I'll just lose it. You know me, it will just get me into trouble. I'm asking you to take it, and do something right with it. I'm asking you as a friend. Most of all, I'm hoping that you still are my friend."

My eyes started to sting. I could hardly see through the tears of joy and relief. I hadn't lost my friend after all. Or her respect. Cilla wasn't there, but everyone else was. They all congratulated me, all happy to see things were right again between us.

It was a good Christmas.

It was the best Christmas I ever had.

I didn't yet know it would be the best Christmas I would ever have.

BACK TO ANABEL

- 35 -

"That's enough story for now," Grandma told me. "I think I've talked more in one day than the last three years combined."

"Just a little more," I pleaded. "We're just getting to the good part."

She said, "You're the first person to tell me these old memories were any good at all. I've shut them away a long time. I never thought I'd have reason to drag them back out. But that's enough for one day. It's getting late. What time is your dinner?"

"Dinner's at 6:30," I said. It was almost 7:00. I quickly added, "But Mom hardly notices me, except to help. It's not like I'm Sammy. He never has to work. He gets rewarded just for not peeing his bed."

"Maybe your mother trusts you more," she said.

I hadn't thought about that.

She said, "You need to go. Do they know where you are?"

They didn't. If they knew, they might not let me come back.

I headed for the door. "I'll be back next Friday," I said. "Don't go anywhere."

"I'll be here," she said. "Waiting for another tomato."

I raced home as fast as I could, worried that when I got home late for dinner, I'd be grounded for a week with no tv or desert. I peeled the door back, hoping I just might sneak in without being noticed.

"Just in time," said Mom. "Dinner's later tonight since we have visitor joining us. Help me put out the good plates."

It turned out the visitor was a lawyer Dad had invited over. I didn't know why because right after dinner, Mom told Sammy and I to go to bed early.

"I wasn't being naughty!" Sammy wailed. "Why do I have to go to my room?"

"You're not being punished," Mom explained. "The grown-ups need some space. We need to talk."

I didn't mind. I was glad to go to my room and shut the door. Grandma's stories twirled in my head, and I wanted time alone to dance with them in my mind.

It was late in the night when I finally fell asleep, a smile of wonder etched onto my face.

By the next morning, the lawyer was gone. I noticed right away that Mom smiled more at Sammy, if that was possible. Like she had a secret, too. As for Dad, he seemed even colder around me and averted his eyes.

It didn't matter. I had my own adult all to myself.

The days stretched on but Friday finally came around again. I could hardly wait to hear what happened next.

But when I got to Grandma's room, I found her door locked.

"It's me," I called, knocking as loud as I could. "Is your door stuck?"

No answer came. A cold knot of fear took hold in my stomach. I pounded on the door, but nothing happened.

I ran down the hall to get Miss Belinda from the front desk.

"You have to come quick," I told her. "Grandma's door is locked and she's not answering. She might be hurt!"

Miss Belinda grabbed a ring of keys and rushed back with me. She tried one key after another, jiggling and joggling then in the keyhole without any luck. Finally, one of the keys clicked. She turned the knob and we went in.

There, in the middle of the room, Grandma sat in her chair. But she didn't see us. She looked past us, her mind somewhere else. Wherever it was, I could see it wasn't a good place.

"I'll call the doctor," said Miss Belinda.

"No," Grandma said. "I'm not sick. There's no medicine for this."

Miss Belinda seemed confused. I was afraid she would make me leave.

Finally, she said to Grandma, "I'm leaving the door open. I'll be right down the hall." Then to me she said, "Maybe you can cheer her up."

I waited until she had left. Then I stood before Grandma.

"What happened?" I asked.

She seemed to fold in on herself. She looked smaller than ever in that big vinyl chair.

When she finally spoke, even her voice sounded tiny. "I signed the papers," she said. "I didn't know. I couldn't find my glasses, and the way he said it, I thought it was for both of you. It wasn't until afterwards that I found out."

"I don't understand. What papers?"

"Your father came by. I told him I wanted to stay right here. He said he wouldn't send me away to somewhere else, as long as I signed the papers. You see, Abner made him the trustee. I thought it was for both of you, so I signed. It wasn't until later that I found out. It all goes to your brother. My house, all of Abner's investments. Your brother gets the whole lot -- you don't get a penny. I have nothing to give you."

She looked so lost and alone.

I saw her orange blanket on her bed and wrapped it around her. "I don't want your old house," I said. "I've got the best part of you right here."

I wanted to hear more of her story, but with everybody taking things from her, this didn't seem like the time.

Instead, I sat on the footstool beside her. We both looked out the window, since she didn't have a tv. We watched a squirrel run across the grass, then we saw it climb up a skinny tree.

She didn't seem to feel like talking and I didn't want to push her.

We didn't say anything at all, we just watched that squirrel for a very long time.

ANABEL TAKES A STAND

- 36 -

I told Grandma I'd be back next week, and left before she could tell me not to.

That night when I got back home, I set the table for diner as usual. I promised myself to act as if nothing had happened so my parents wouldn't know where I'd been. I was going to be cool, and keep my secret to myself.

Dad came in for dinner and Mom dished up the food and we all sat down. But Dad didn't seem like his normal angry self. He looked smug. I could see him and Mom exchanging glances. They looked so pleased with themselves, like they'd done something worth being proud of.

It made me so angry the words just leapt out of my mouth.

"I know what you did," I said. "How could you? You took everything from her."

"Anabel," Mom snapped. "You do NOT speak to your parents like that."

I glared back. "How should I speak to parents? Make them sign papers so they've got nothing left, like you did with your Grandma?"

Mom turned so red she looked sunburned. Dad's fork dropped on his plate with a clatter. I was sure they'd banish me with no tv forever.

Mom turned to Sammy. "Samuel, you don't need to hear this. You should go upstairs right now."

"Me?" he cried. "What did I do?"

"Why shouldn't he hear it?" I said. "After all, it all goes to him. What you tricked out of her."

"Go!" Mom said to Sammy. "Now!"

I'd never heard Mom use that tone with Sammy before. He hadn't either, and he ran upstairs as fast as his legs would go.

Mom turned to me, her eyes spitting fire. "Look what you've done," she said. "You've upset your brother."

"But it's okay for you to upset *her*?"

Dad said, "Whatever she tells you, remember the source. My mother has mental issues. I spent most of my childhood without a mother around because she was off in an institution -- *again*."

This was the first whiff I had heard of that, but it didn't stop my anger. "Are you saying you *didn't* make her sign papers to give away her house and everything else?"

Both Dad and Mom went very quiet. Mom looked at Dad.

He gathered his thoughts, then he said, "You want the truth? Life is hard. We're just getting by, paying the bills. I'd like to send both you kids off to college, when the time comes. But that's not likely. Your grandfather made me executor of his estate -- one of the few things he ever did for me. With the nursing home fees, there's not going to be much left. Anabel, your mother tells me you often talk back, and that your mind is off in the clouds, watching shows on tv or what-not. We've decided that between you and your brother, it's Samuel that deserves a chance."

"Not a penny goes to us," Mom added. "It all goes into a college trust fund, for when he turns 18."

"It's not his money," I said. "That's not fair."

Dad said, "I was sent away from home as soon as I could walk. Was that fair? Now I work hard for our family, and should be making more than I do, but my job's not fair. Your mother would like to have more children, but the doctor says Samuel will be her last baby. Life never promised us 'fair,' Anabel. Not for us, not for you. We do our best with what we have. That's all we can do."

Dad had never spoken to me that way before, what was really on his mind. Now I understood why he looked so stressed most of the time. And why Mom babied Sammy.

Was it true, that Grandma was crazy? Was everything she said make-believe?

I looked at my Mom.

She nodded. "Yes," she said. "You can go up to your room now. I think we've all said enough for one night." Then she added, "Take your plate. I don't want you going to sleep hungry. I'll bring one up for your brother."

*

That was a very long week. I had a lot of thinking to do. At the same time, I worried they'd forbid me from seeing Grandma again.

But they didn't say any more about it, and I didn't bring it up. It was like we all pretended that conversation never happened.

But sometimes I would notice Dad looking my way with a thoughtful look on his face. I'd never seen him like that before, and I didn't dare catch his eye. Whatever those thoughts of his were, I didn't want to chase them away.

When the next Friday rolled around, I made sure I was ready. My homework for the weekend was already done by the time I got home. As soon as I got off the bus, I announced I would be going outside.

Mom didn't stop me. She didn't say anything at all.

But she handed me a brown paper bag. In it I saw a fat ripe tomato.

I guess something had changed in us all. When I got to Grandma's room, she also seemed different.

At first, she seemed surprised to see me. Then she looked away and said, "They told you I was crazy, didn't they."

I didn't have to answer; she already knew it.

She said, "Do you believe them?"

I shrugged. I'd spent a lot of time thinking about that. I'd tried to remember every crazy person I'd seen in the movies, even though I knew they were only pretending. I didn't know what a real crazy person looked like. How could I?

"It doesn't matter," she said. "The story's over anyway."

"You can't stop now!" I gasped. "What about Christmas?"

She said, "Buffalo Bill died two weeks later, in January of 1917. America couldn't stay out of the big war and our boys started dying over in Europe. People were jumpy, even scared of the mailman with those awful letters that started popping up -- the *We-Regret-To-Inform-You*'s. Times had changed. The west wasn't wild anymore. It was the end."

"It wasn't the end of you," I said. "You can't stop there. What about your horse? What about Glory's garden, and the look on Cilla's face when you bought Dusty Blue?"

"It's over," she said. "Go home and leave me alone."

"You have the right to be angry at my Dad," I said. "But don't take it out on me."

"Can't you see?" she told me. "I'm tired of fighting. I just can't do it any more."

It wasn't until that moment that I realized just how important my Grandma was to me, and not just for her stories. Our time was special, like when we watched the squirrel and didn't even need to talk.

I was dangerously close to losing all that.

"You don't have to say anything," I told her, "but I'm not leaving. You're the only adult who's been on my side all the way, and that's worth fighting for, isn't it?"

She didn't say anything for a long time. It got so quiet I could hear my heart thump in my chest.

At last she spoke. "You know, in all my years, I have never told anyone all the pieces. Maybe I should. Maybe it is finally time."

I nodded my head. "You can tell me," I said. "After Christmas that year, what happened next?"

THE NEW YEAR 1917

- 37 -

It was a brand new year, the start of 1917. According to Lill I was awfully close to having the $250 to buy Dusty Blue. We figured one or two more good batches of mending would put me over the top. I packed my basket of mending supplies to go into town, wondering if this would be the trip that would help me reach my goal.

Cilla didn't know how close I was. She had no idea, and Rosey said we should keep it that way. She said it would be fun to spring it on Cilla all at once when I had the full amount, and announce it in front of all the girls. Rosey and I wondered what color would Cilla's face turn. Would she gasp like a catfish out of water? Would she simmer or stammer or stomp her feet like a child? Picturing Cilla's reaction was almost as much fun as imagining my first ride on my very own Dusty Blue.

Full of our secret, Rosey and I giggled like fools as we hitched the horses to the wagon shafts, with Big Red on the right with Klara's Lady on the left. Even the weather bent to our mood as the sun lifted its head from behind a cloud, and burned a hole in the winter chill. It was a sign, Rosey said, that today would be a good day.

I didn't know at the time that joy comes with a cost. All I knew was that Klara and Violet were packing the wagon with heaps of laundry and baskets of pies, and taking their sweet time doing the job.

Rosey thought so, too. "You could pack a lot faster," she told Violet, "if you wore pants like the rest of us instead of that big swishy shirt."

"We could pack faster," Violet answered, "if you and Maisy would help. Just because your gear is already loaded doesn't mean you can't lend us a hand."

Rosey and I laughed because Violet was right.

But mostly we laughed because it felt good. At that moment, everything felt good.

Once we'd hoisted up all the hampers and boxes, the wagon was so full there was barely room for us. I squeezed into the front seat with Rosey while Klara and Violet perched on boxes in the back.

"You really think you can sell all of those pies?" Rosey asked.

"If not we can trade them for store credit," said Klara. "We are almost out of supplies."

Rosey turned to Violet, trying hard to look dainty perched on a stack of crates. "Speaking of lists, how is your other list coming? Any luck yet with any of those church boys?"

"Mind your own business," said Violet.

"This is my business," Rosey replied. "I need to know if I'll be dropping you off at the store or the church."

"Just the store," said Violet. "God's house isn't open on Wednesday. You'd know that if you went once in a while."

Before Rosey could snap off a reply, Cilla came tearing out of the bunk house.

"Wait up," she cried, stuffing her arms into her red going-to-town corduroy jacket. "I'm coming, too!"

Rosey shook her head. "Not this time. We've got a big list of supplies to pick up and we'll be coming back heavy. We can't take on any more weight. You'll have to stay in camp with Glory and Lill."

"Don't be silly," said Cilla. "There's plenty of room for me."

"You didn't help load," said Rosey. "You got no right to come on this trip."

Cilla climbed into the wagon anyway, and wedged herself

between two boxes so tightly that there was no way we could pry her off.

"I'll make sure nothing falls out," she said. "See? I'm helping already."

There was no getting around it. We were stuck with her.

I jumped down from the driver's bench. "You all go ahead. I'll saddle up one of the horses and catch up with you on the way."

"You sure?" Rosey asked.

I nodded. Then I looked towards the corral. Dusty Blue stood at the edge, watching like a wistful child who had to stay home from the fair. He saw me get off the wagon, and nodded his head up and down, pleased. Rosey noticed and smiled.

Cilla saw it, too. "Oh, no you don't," she said. "Maisy, don't even think of riding my horse. You have your own horse. That spackled thing. You ride her."

"That's not very generous," said Violet, "seeing how Maisy gave up her space on the wagon for you."

Cilla frowned. "It's not that I don't appreciate it. But Dusty Blue's not some old hack horse, only good for hauling people around. He's a professional trick riding horse, finely-tuned to my commands. As long as I'll be riding him in the shows, I can't have that jeopardized. That's just the way it is."

Rosey opened her mouth to reply, but instead, she grinned and snapped the reins. The wagon bolted away.

"Wait," Cilla cried out. "I'm not done speaking my peace. Maisy, I FORBID you to ride my horse. Do you hear me? You can't ride him. You can't..."

Her voice trailed off as the wagon surged away, and I laughed at the sight of her growing smaller and smaller, her arms still flapping and flailing. She couldn't stop me now. Why shouldn't I ride him? He was almost mine.

I opened the corral gate and let him out. I didn't need to tie him onto a lead rope. He knew where to go, and he pranced along beside me all the way to the stable wall where the bridles were kept.

There they were, all lined up. Thunder's bridle with the sliver buckles. Spackle's bit with the rope-knit set of reins. Even the riding collar I made for Sugar, Klara's cow.

But Dusty Blue's bridle was gone. It wasn't on the floor, or on another peg. It just wasn't there. His mouth was too big for any of the others to fit.

Cilla had skunked me after all. Darn that girl.

I nestled my face against Dusty Blue's neck, and brushed his mane with my hand. "Sorry, boy. It's too far to ride without a bridle. I'll have to take Spackles after all."

He looked at me and sadly bobbed his head. Then he walked back to the corral, waiting for me to let him back in.

WHAT CILLA GOT UP TO

- 38 -

Rosey stopped the wagon first at the tailor's shop. Klara got out with a basket of clothes.

"It looks awfully heavy," said Violet. "Need some help?"

Klara shook her head. "I can deliver this load by myself, and pick up the mending for Maisy. Then I will come help you at the store."

Rosey drove the wagon away. Two blocks later, Rosey pulled up alongside the General Store. There Violet unloaded the pie hampers and the empty crates. Cilla got off the wagon, but didn't help unload. She always had some reason not to, and this time was no different.

Rosey said to Violet, "I've got to go trim the Slater's horses. That won't take me too long. I should be back pretty soon, unless they got those new ponies they've been talking about. If they did, it might take me a while."

"Take your time," said Violet. "I'll be here and ready when you're done."

Violet handed Cilla a piece of paper. "Here's the grocery list," Violet said. "At least you can go ahead and start the order while I drop off these pies. Whatever you do, don't lose that list."

Cilla tucked the list into her pocket. "Sure. I'll be there in a minute. I just need to do something first, on the other side of the street."

"No," said Violet. "We need to get this order filled. There's nothing on the other side of the street but the saloon."

"You've got your business," said Cilla, "and I've got mine. You all agreed you needed me for publicity, remember?"

Violet said, "You said you were coming to help. We're not doing any shows now until Spring. Taking off on your own is not helping one bit."

Cilla said, "I'll be back before you know it."

"What about our supplies?" Violet called after her.

Cilla kept going.

Violet stomped her foot. "If you're not back in time, I'm going to let Rosey leave town without you."

Cilla grinned; she didn't even turn around as she headed across the street towards the Moab saloon.

*

Cilla spotted the man in the black coat right away. She'd never seen him before, she was sure of that. He was quite striking with a mane of silver hair that brushed the shoulders of his coat, an expensive coat from the cut of it but well-worn.

She wouldn't hold that against him. She always did like a man in a fine cut of cloth.

He was alone at the bar. She sidled up next to him, but he ignored her, lost in his thoughts.

She tapped her feet, impatient for him to pull out a chair for her.

When he didn't, she cleared her throat. "I can tell you're new here, since you obviously don't know who I am."

"Should I?" he asked.

"I should say so," she answered. "Everyone in this town knows who I am. I'm a celebrity around here. My name's Priscilla, but that's Cilla to you. I'm the top draw of the Little Darlin's Wild West Show. The All-Girl No-Man Little Darlin's Wild Wild West -- the greatest show you'll ever see."

"The Little Darlin's?" he said, a sudden interest sparking his eyes. "Are you one of them?"

"The best of the bunch. You could say I'm the queen bee. The rest are all my little drones. They do what I say."

"Tell me," he said, pulling a photo from his vest pocket. "Do you know this girl?"

Cilla studied the tattered photograph. There was a single figure, head tipped down, making it a hard to make out the face.

But Cilla didn't need to see the face to know. The posture was unmistakable. As was the girl's hair, as light as corn silk.

"Maybe I do and maybe I don't," Cilla said. "Who wants to know?"

The man's eyes narrowed. "You have seen her, haven't you?"

Cilla examined the long, lean stranger. Was this the husband? He looked too old for that. His hair was pure silver, and such a glossy shade it might once have been gold.

"You're Glory's father," she said.

He gasped a breath.

Cilla smiled. "Of course, you are," she said. "You've got her nose. She's not in trouble, is she? For running away from her husband?"

"No, she... what did you say?"

"For running away from that no-good husband of hers. The one who beat her."

"Glory told you that?"

"She didn't have to. I just know. A woman's intuition, you might say."

He thought a moment before replying. "You are very astute," He said. "Her mother and I have been worried sick. You can't imagine how hard it is for your daughter to just disappear like that. It's a parent's worst fear..." He stopped and placed his hand on her arm. "Ah, but an intelligent, attractive young girl like yourself doesn't need to worry about things like that."

Cilla giggled.

"I know you'll help me," he said.

"Well, I don't know..."

"She's not strong and brave, like you," he told her. "My daughter is... fragile."

"Isn't that the truth!"

He nodded. "She needs to be protected. You can't keep her safe forever. It's not your job. For her own sake, you have to tell me where she is. It's only right. Besides, I'm prepared to make it worth your while."

"How much is my while worth?" Cilla asked.

"What do you want?"

"What are you offering?"

He flipped down a bill. Then another.

Cilla said nothing, stalling for time. The longer she kept him waiting, the more money he threw into the pile.

But really, there was nothing to decide. Her mind was already firm.

Silly man, Cilla thought, as the reward pile kept growing. Didn't he know Glory never belonged in the show? As far as Cilla was concerned, getting rid of Glory was reward enough.

LAST TRIP TO MOAB

- 41 -

That day, Spackles was as ornery as I'd ever seen her. She didn't want to be caught and she flat-out refused to behave. By the time I got her saddled and headed towards town, it was so late I thought I might meet the wagon coming back.

I didn't. I found the wagon at the General Store. Klara was packing eggs around the new batch of mending she'd picked up from the hotel, while Violet and Rosey were loading the crates. Cilla sat in the wagon, getting in the way, not helping at all.

"You're still here?" I said to Rosey. "You must have been busy. I guess the Slaters got those new horses after all."

"Oh, he got them, all right," she said. "But they're Mustangs. Desert horses, with hooves as tough as nails. Don't need any shoeing at all. No, it wasn't me that held us up." She made a face towards Cilla.

"Cilla lost the grocery list," said Violet with a sigh. "We've been wracking our brains to remember what all was on it. Honestly, Cilla. Where could it have gone?"

"Never mind about that," said Cilla. "I've been here in town helping, which is more than I can for Maisy. Why don't you ask what took *her* so long?"

"Spackles was in a mood," I said, patting my lazy horse's rump. Rosey was about to ask why I hadn't taken Dusty Blue, but I shook my head, cutting her off. *Tell you later.*

Cilla said, "It's not *my* fault Maisy can't control her own horse."

"If you let her ride yours," said Rosey, "she *would've* been her sooner."

"And maybe," said Cilla, "if she was a better rider, she wouldn't *need* to ride mine."

"Will you two just stop it?" said Violet. "Can't we do one thing, just one little trip into town without all this bickering? Honestly!"

No one said anything else. I dropped down from Spackles to help pack the last crates onto the wagon. By the time we were done, the wagon groaned from the weight. I'd never seen it loaded so heavy.

We set out from Moab across the red rock in a slow, steady pace. I rode alongside on Spackles who behaved herself now, not wanting to be left behind.

THE STRANGER AGAIN

- 40 -

The man in the long coat approached the Mother Lode Camp from the south. He paused on his horse one last time to study the paper in hand -- the folded sheet the loud woman had given him with a grocery list on the front. On the back, she'd drawn a map to make sure he found his way to where Glory was hiding.

It was providence, he felt, that put the loud woman in his path. A sign that what he was doing was right.

He'd come a long way to find his daughter. Soon it would all be worth it.

He nudged his horse on, each clip-clop of the hooves now bringing him closer to his goal. So much searching. So many miles. Soon they'd be together again, where she belonged.

He had to protect her from the world, from all of its evils. As her father, it was his job to keep her from all the things she might be tempted to do. The horses' clip-clopping seemed to be calling her name -- Glo-ry, Glo-ry, Glo-ry, Glo-ry.

She was his baby, his precious little girl.

Glory was even more precious to him now, to find out she hadn't told anyone what had transpired between them.

He'd suffered so much worry, wondering what stories might had spilled from her pretty lips. What confused tales she might have planted along her way.

What a relief, to find she hadn't said anything at all.

But for all the worry she'd caused him, she'd have to atone for that.

Perhaps she had learned her lesson, he thought. Maybe this time things would be different. If only she would not tempt him with her womanly shape, her body so lush and ripe.

Yet as soon as those thoughts entered his head, he was flooded with desire. He began to quiver, then to shake.

Unable to stop the torrent, he was forced to dismount, He ducked behind a boulder and relieved his desire behind it.

When the tide had spilled from him, it gave him no joy. It only left him shaken by the violence of it.

How selfish of her, to cast such a hold on him. He had come prepared to forgive her for the past. Despite his goodwill, she still exerted her evil ways on his soul. It was perverse, to crave the flesh of your flesh. A sin against God.

But it wasn't his sin. He was a victim, like Adam, seduced by Eve. Eve had been made from Adam's own rib, to honor and assist. But Eve had been wanton, and taught Adam to desire and led him astray.

Just as Glory led him into darkness and shame. He'd given her life -- he'd grown her from his own precious seed. Yet her body tormented him and led him astray. Even now, just thinking of her, her devilish form tempted him into forbidden thoughts.

She would have to pay for that. It had gone on long enough. This time, there would be no room for weakness. The curse she put on him must be lifted at all costs. To end the torture, the evil would have to be stopped. Not only to save his soul, but to purify hers.

For her own sake, the abomination that had claimed Glory's spirit would have to be purged.

A TRUTH BETRAYED

- 41 -

Cilla's grin was relentless. I thought it was because of the way she had scooped me from riding her horse.

I tried to ignore her. Dusty Blue would be mine soon enough.

We were just a few miles from camp when Cilla pulled out a bottle of cider and offered it around.

Violet took a swig, then passed it to Klara. "Not bad," Violet said. "What's got into you, Cilla? Sharing isn't your specialty."

"How can you say that?" said Cilla. "You're living in my mining camp. How much more hospitable could I be? Besides, can't I feel happy to be with my rodeo pals? We all deserve to be here. Even you, Rosey, who always argues with me. And Maisy who only likes me for my horse. Every one of you is a true blue cowgirl. A real Little Darlin of the wild west. Not many people can say that."

"I'll drink to that," said Rosey. "Where's that bottle?"

"Stop the wagon right now," said Cilla. "Maisy, get in here, too. Let's have a toast. To us. To being cowgirls like this, forever and ever."

I was feeling so good I agreed. Who was I to stop a good time? The winter sun felt warm on my skin, the air crisp and dry. It was a fine day. This was what being a cowgirl was all about -- life's little joys that took us by surprise. I could almost forgive Cilla everything she'd done to put a shine on a moment like that.

Rosey pulled the wagon to a halt. I hitched Spackles to the side and climbed in to join the others. Just as I was about to sit down on a crate, I heard a sound. It was the shrill cry of a horse in the distance.

A shiver of fear ran up my spine.

"Did you hear that?" I said.

"Hear what?" Rosey asked.

"A horse in trouble," I said. "Could be one of ours."

"Don't be ridiculous," said Cilla. "Nobody can hear this far away. We're two miles from camp, at least."

I heard it again. "There!" I said.

Cilla frowned. "Maisy, stop acting like you've got special powers. You know you're just being a fool."

Violet said, "What happened to just being happy with your friends?"

"Yeah," said Rosey. "Cilla, you're acting awfully cagey. Why did you want us to stop?"

"Me?" she snapped. "I'm not the one who hears voices that aren't there. What is it, Maisy? Your father again? That story about how he told you to run *after* he was dead? Are you hearing ghosts again?"

It always hurt when Cilla brought up my Papa like that. She had a way of making the pain fresh all over again.

Violet looked at her. "Cilla. You were in that saloon an awfully long time. Who gave you that bottle? What happened in there?"

"Yeah," said Rosey. "And why did you insist we stop here, before we got to camp? What are you up to?"

"Leave me alone," said Cilla. "Lill won't like you all ganging up on me."

Violet said, "Lill is not here. This time you can't hide behind her big furry pants."

"All right," Cilla said. "You're going to find out soon enough. I might as well tell you now. Yes, I did talk to someone in the saloon. It was her father."

"Whose father?" said Rosey.

"Glory's. He's been worried sick, the poor man. He's traveled hundreds of miles just to find her. So of course I told him where she was. He's probably at the camp collecting her right now, to bring her home. I imagine she'll be making a scene as he hauls her off. Who wants to see that? You should be thanking me."

There as a stunned silence as we glared at her.

"You don't understand," said Cilla. "The man was in pain."

"You promised," said Violet. "We made a pact we wouldn't tell anyone. You gave your word -- your word as a *cowgirl*."

"Glory's not a cowgirl," said Cilla. "She doesn't even have an act. Sure, she rode the bronc. But it was only one time. Don't you see? She never belonged. Let her father deal with her from now on. Let him keep her from that no-good husband who beat her."

I didn't know what to say. None of us did.

It was Klara who saw through it. "Glory never said it was her husband who beat her."

"Of course it was," Cilla insisted. "Those bruises were layered deep, we all saw them. Not from some dude passing by, they came from someone she knew a long, long time. Who else...?"

We all got it at once -- me, Rosey, Vi, and Klara. Even Cilla finally saw it.

I jumped off the wagon right onto Spackles' back. I didn't even untie her rope, I just cut it off and lit out of there.

As I took off, I saw Rosey unhooking Big Red. She knew, as I did, that a horse with a rider was faster than a wagon any day.

I didn't see what else happened behind me after that.

I didn't see Violet, who hated to ride, climb up behind Rosey on the back of Big Red.

I didn't see Klara take the wagon reins, with only Lady pulling it now, and drive that cart so hard and so fast that our tools and supplies spilled out behind it like a trail of trash.

I didn't see Cilla screaming at Klara to slow down, or Cilla trying to grapple the reins from Klara's grip.

And I didn't see Klara give Cilla a swift shove, knocking our trick rider off of the wagon, to hit the dirt and bounce across the red hardpan like a broken rag doll.

Of all of the terrible things that happened that day, that was the only thing I didn't see that I wished that I had.

THE DANGER OF STRANGERS

- 42 -

Lill came up from the barn and met Glory by the cookhouse door. "Dusty Blue's acting spooked," said Lill. "Like he does before a storm. It must be a big one from the way he's acting, all pacing and snorting and getting the others riled up. I penned them all up safe in the barn."

"I hope the girls get back before it hits," said Glory. "Funny, I don't see any rain clouds."

"Could be a dust storm, for all we know. We'd better make sure the windows are shut tight, just in case. You take the cook shack. I'll close up the bunk house."

Glory nodded and nipped back into the cook shack. Lill headed down the path towards the bunk house. She looked up at the sky and smiled to herself. Glory was right -- it looked like a beautiful day.

Behind her she heard a branch snap. She jumped.

"Hello, there, Miss. I believe I'm lost. Can you help me?"

It was just a skinny old fellow, on foot, blown off of his course. Lill laughed out loud for being startled by something as harmless as that. "Well, I suppose I might can help you," she said. "It depends on where you're trying to get."

"Is this the Mother Lode Mining Camp?"

As the man drew near, she thought there was something familiar about him. Something about the way that he talked, or the stretch of his limbs. Lill tilted her head, squinting in the sun to figure it out.

"I said, is this the Mother Lode Camp?" he repeated. "What's wrong with you, girl? Didn't you hear me the first time? You need to learn to answer your betters."

Lill planted her feet, her hands on her hips. "First of all, mister, I ain't your girl. Second of all, you're nobody's 'better' and third, you ain't been invited..."

He snapped out a pistol and rammed the butt end into her skull with a loud *CLASH*. She crumpled to the ground like a dry autumn leaf.

Glory heard the noise. She came running out of the cook shack and stopped cold at the sight of Lill's body sprawled on the ground.

Her father stood over Lill, his eyes as cold as the gun-metal in his hands.

"What have you done?" Glory cried. She ran to Lill's body and cradled Lill's head in her arms. "Lill! Wake up! It's me he's after, not you. Don't die on me, Lill. Please, don't. Please!"

"I didn't want it to be like this," he said. "No one was supposed to get hurt. This was between you and me. But you had to make it hard. You had to run away. Now look at the damage you've wrought."

"YOU did this," she said. "This isn't my fault."

"Come with me now," he said, "and no one else has to suffer."

"You have no right," she said. "I'm a married woman now."

He laughed. "That boy up in Butte? That wasn't a real marriage. It was a sham. An excuse for you to run away. Then you ran from him, too. I had it annulled. You know what that means? It means you're still mine. Glory, it's time to come home."

"I won't go back with you," she said. "Not as long as I live."

He sighed. "I was afraid you'd say that." He pointed his pistol at her head.

"Go ahead," she said. "Shoot. Then everyone will know just like I do what an animal you are."

"There's no one here but us," he said. "Ah, Glory. Such a waste. You were given a gift, child. The gift of beauty. But you used it to entice. To spin your evil web."

"I never did that," she said. "You're a monster. I didn't want you."

"So your words say. But I know better. This is for your own good. A blessing. So your beauty will never seduce another man, a man created in HIS image. You'll never steal another man's soul again, or tempt his manhood -- his *God-hood*, into your unworthy self. Prepare yourself, woman. Prepare to greet your maker to make amends."

Glory held Lill in her arms and closed her eyes to what was to come.

He leaned down above her and brought his gun so close that the barrel touched her forehead. He caressed the trigger, stroking it gently, feeling the power throb gloriously in his hand.

Then a new throbbing washed through him. It was a familiar ache but stronger than ever before.

Just one more time, he told himself. The very last time.

He sunk to his knees. He pushed Lill's body aside and pinned Glory beneath him, his gun still in hand. She deserved this, for all she'd put him through. He'd suffered so much to find her. This was his right. His due.

Then came the sound of repeated thumping.

He tried to ignore it but it wouldn't stop. The noise was everywhere, bouncing like drumbeats off the camp's walls.

Glory opened her eyes. "The storm," she said. "It's here."

He listened as the thumping gave way to a shattering sound. Thunder against wood. It was not natural. Not human.

"Can you hear it father? This is no rain storm. This is the storm of God, and it's coming for you."

Fear shot through him, but it didn't stop his need. Like pouring fuel on a fire, it ignited his loins even stronger. He tore free of his trousers and ripped her clothes from her legs.

The pounding sound increased, as if urging him on. With it came the searing cry of a horse.

"The four horsemen cometh!" he cried, gasping between breaths. "The apocalypse is nigh. Like Jacob before me, I give the most sacred sacrifice, the child of my flesh. Let me become the blade of your taking. Let my body be the sword that delivers this soiled lamb unto you."

She struggled beneath him, but he was so much stronger -- and filled with insane vigor as he fell on her again and again.

A gray shape loomed overhead -- the rearing of hooves.

"They're here," he grunted. "The rapture cometh... Use me... Oh, use me..."

"Get him!" said Glory.

The man looked up. It was no apocalyptic vision above him.

It was just a horse. A lowly gray beast of burden. It reared on its hind legs above him, as if trying to attack him, but unable to commit.

The man watched spell-bound to see a thousand pounds of frenzied horse flesh rearing overhead -- but unable to stomp him, rendered just as powerless as the soiled lamb pinned under his legs.

Oh, the power of a divine mission.

As the man continued plummeting into his treasure, he began to understand.

The horse, helplessly pawing the air, was trying to protect the girl. But it knew that to come down on the man would crush the girl, too.

The man smiled. Now he knew -- just as Glory was his, the taking of this horse-flesh creature was his manly right, too.

The man reached up towards the horse, the gun still in hand. He aimed at the soft underbelly between the animal's legs, so perfectly exposed.

And he fired.

As the bullet met its mark, the man's tension also released. His back arched up in exquisite elation.

As for the horse, it was propelled up by the impact. It contracted and twisted in the air, its last act a deliberate feat to fall away from the girl.

As the horse fell to the earth, the man collapsed too, now at last fully gorged on the feast of his lust.

ON THE EDGE

- 43 -

A horse will always run faster heading towards home. I
hunched into Spackles, spurring her on with every ounce of my fear.
We flew like the wind. I could hear Big Red not far behind.

I don't know how long it took. I don't remember that.

I only knew there was only one thought shuddering through my
mind.

Run!

I rounded the turn into camp just as the shot rang out, the single
cold blast, just in time to see Dusty Blue flung up high, and twist, and
land in the dirt.

Spackles stopped dead in a panic.

I went over her head like a ball shot from a cannon. I curled
into the fall, and hit the ground like a rolling ball.

When I finally stopped rolling, I lifted my head, stunned to see
that I was still in one piece. Then I saw the man rise to his feet, his gun
pointed at me.

I stood up and ran towards him, desperate to get to the gray
horse on the ground.

A shot came from behind.

The bullet whipped past me.

The man's hand exploded, his gun falling away. His fingers
dangled, bloody and useless.

It had to be Violet. The only one I knew who could pull off that
shot.

I ran on towards the scene. The man now held his stump of a wrist, trying to stem the red flow.

Then I was there with Dusty Blue, sprawled on his side, his eyes white with fear.

I felt his big horse head below me, pink froth splurting from his throat. His breath raw and ragged.

I blew into his nose. I tried to breathe for him.

Tears rained onto his head. I willed my strength to him, like a fairy tale princess whose salt tears bring life.

Dusty Blue's eyes rolled back, then his mouth opened sideways. Out came one final blast of sweet feed.

Papa, don't leave me again.

I saw Lill's body off to the side.

And Glory, her clothes shredded and covered in filth. She dragged herself to her feet, and picked up the gun that fell from the man's busted hand.

The man, now on his knees, knelt before Glory. He whimpered in pain. He begged her. He pleaded.

A voice came from behind. "I've got a bead on him, Glory. He can't hurt you anymore."

Then another voice. "Don't do it, bronc rider. He ain't worth it."

And Glory shaking her head.

She aimed the gun for his right knee.

"This one's for Lill."

Bang!

She targeted his left knee.

"This one's for me."

Bang!

Then she honed in on his chest.

"And this one's for Dusty Blue."

AFTER THE RUSH

- 44 -

Miraculously, Lill woke up, not a scratch on her, but she had the king of all headaches. She couldn't remember anything that had happened, and at the time, that seemed like a blessing.

Spackles ran off. She must have bolted out of camp after I went over her head. She'd probably been waiting all this time for one good chance to escape, so that's what she did.

We never found her. Not a trace, not a piece. Odds are, with her bridle gear still on, she got snagged in the brush and dragged off by a wild cat or a pack of wolves.

But maybe she got free. Maybe she was smarter than I ever gave her credit for. After all, she was right all along, not to trust humans. Because some humans are worse than animals – they kill for reasons other than food. Maybe, just maybe, somewhere out there, her colors still dot the badlands -- whole generations of persnickety horses so shy, and so sly, that nobody's ever seen them.

But there was no pretending with Dusty Blue. He was dead. He'd died a hero's death.

We dug a big hole out back in a grassy patch and laid him to rest. It was the last thing we did as a team, the last time the Little Darlin's were all together.

All together minus one.

A rider heading south found Cilla, and carted her off to La Sal. She had broken plenty of bones, but her mouth worked well enough to tell the town sheriff what she knew. She said Klara had pushed her out of the wagon. So he came out to arrest Klara for assault. He got more than he bargained for when he found Glory's father shot full of holes.

We'd left the old coot right where he fell -- didn't even bother to cover him, even when the crows picked away at his parts.

We told Sheriff the story. We thought he would help us. But he arrested Violet and Glory and took them in, too.

"Formalities," he said. "If your story holds up, and this was really self-defense, I'll have your friends back in no time."

That left just Rosey, Lill, and me back at the camp. Our supplies had been scattered out the back of the wagon so we had no food. Lill, who had kept all our money, couldn't remember where it was. There was a lot of things she couldn't remember anymore.

With our remaining horses, we rode back to the trail where Cilla fell out. Rosey went looking for Cilla's bottle of cider. Maybe she was hoping it turned hard. I was glad she didn't find it.

Nearly all of our supplies were gone, blown away or scavenged by critters. We did find some onions and beans. We boiled some up into soup and lived off of that.

It was quiet at the camp. Rosey and I didn't have anything to say and Lill didn't bother. In fact, she didn't say much at all, which wasn't like her. We didn't notice at first. We were just numb.

Two days later the sheriff came back. He had Klara with him, all right, and released her. But he didn't bring Glory or Violet home. Instead he had a whole posse with him.

Cilla couldn't prove Klara pushed her out the wagon with the way the supplies all fell out, so they set Klara free.

But Glory and Vi were still under arrest. There were parts of our story that didn't make sense, according to Sheriff. From what everyone said, Glory's father was a good man. A God-fearing man. They decided to have a big trial up in Salt Lake City, with special lawyers and all. They said this would take a while.

On top of that, they told us the Mother Lode Camp wasn't Cilla's after all. The sheriff found it was owned by some claim-stakers in Reno, and telegraphed them right away. They weren't pleased we'd been living there on their land, and said that we owed them some rent. They demanded a whole pile of money.

We didn't have it, we told Sheriff. There was no way we could pay all of that.

"That's why we're taking your horses," he said. "To sell off at auction."

The sheriff and his boys went out to the corral.

"The brown and the palomino are fine horses," I said. "You'll get plenty for them. And you're welcome to the spackled horse, if you can find her. But leave us the black horse and the red."

"I got to take them all," said the sheriff.

Klara ran inside and hid under the bed. She just couldn't face watching them haul Lady away.

If I was smart, I would have joined her.

I'd never seen Rosey with tears in her eyes. Not even when she lost her house back in Jackson. Not when Glory rode the bronc, or when Lill woke up. Not even when we buried Dusty Blue.

But when they hauled off Big Red, she cried a whole lake.

Klara joined her, when she saw that they'd taken her cow, too.

They were just gone, as if they'd never been with us. As if they'd never existed.

As if we'd never been cowgirls.

SEND IN THE CLOWNS

– 47 –

That's when Klara left. She said she was sick of the U.S. of A and just walked off. We didn't try to stop her. We didn't have the strength. We think she might have gone back to her old country, but we couldn't be sure.

For a week, we wandered around the camp like ghosts, Rosey, Lill, and I. We didn't eat much and we talked even less. Even Lill. That's when we started to realize she wasn't just blue. The damage to her brain went much deeper than that.

Another posse came and hauled us off to Salt Lake, to give our side of the story. The prosecutor was a big bully of a man, while our state-assigned defense lawyer was a weasel named Dempsy Littledink. That was his actual name, although why he would keep it, I'll never know. Anyway, he didn't take kindly to women who shot their own guns and ran their own show. Maybe that's why he was such a useless lawyer for us. Or maybe somebody paid him off.

For days the lawyers asked us questions, poking holes at our stories, asking us things we already told them and things they knew we didn't know. Then they brought in a man with dark eyes. A character witness, they said. He looked like the devil to me. He said Miss Violet Eubanks and Klara stole his horses. He said he had proof. Then he whipped out a letter Violet wrote to him, along with a picture of Lady and dead old Prize with her brand cut off, bleeding all over the street in Montpelier.

I was glad Klara had already left us and had gotten away. She was smart to do that.

They brought in another man. This one was scruffy and nervous, and didn't seem to want to be there any more than we did. He said he gave Glory a horse. A fine specimen that cost him a lot of money. He said she kept the horse but never even thanked him for it. Not one little second of her time.

Then they put me in that box in the courtroom, and made me swear on a bible that everything I said was true. Our lawyer Mr. Littledink asked if Violet shot Glory's father. I tried to say she only shot his gun from his hand but he cut me off. Yes or no, he said, don't say anything else. So I had to say yes. Then he asked me if Glory shot her own father.

"You don't understand," I said.

"Just answer the question," he said. "Did Glory Skaarland shoot her father after he had been wounded by Violet Eubanks?"

"She had to," I said. "Because Glory's father was killing Dusty Blue."

"Are you saying that Mr. Skaarland had no right to protect himself? That he deserved to die because he defended himself against a horse?"

"He was doing more that defending himself," I said. "He tried to shoot me. He aimed his gun right at me."

"But yet you ran towards him, isn't that true, Miss Macedonia Lee? Isn't that what you said before, that you ran *towards* him?"

I nodded.

"Yet why would you run *towards* Mr. Skaarland if he was aiming his gun at you?"

"To save Dusty Blue."

"Miss Lee," said Mr. Littledink. "Do you expect us to believe that if your life was in danger, if you felt you were truly threatened, that you would run *towards* a loaded gun pointed directly at you, in order to save a *horse*?"

He said *horse* like it was a bad word. A creature too lowly for life. I said the only thing I could think of that would make him understand. "Dusty Blue wasn't just a horse. He was a special horse. A registered trick-riding horse. Registered in the trick riding book and everything!"

"A registered... what?" He gaped at me a moment, and then like a fire in a hay barn, that whole room erupted into great gusts of laughter, with our stinking little weasel of a lawyer laughing hardest of all. I felt sick to my stomach, to see all those people, who weren't even there, making fun of the one creature that gave his life to save Glory. To save me.

For that moment alone, if Cilla hadn't done anything else rotten, to me it seemed more than enough for a one-way ticket to eternal flames.

Needless to say, that miserable Mr. Littledink did not 'prove' that Glory's father cracked Lill's skull. Or even that the father attacked Glory. We hadn't actually seen any of that happen with our eyes. Not me, or Rosey, or Violet.

Lill had seen it, but she couldn't remember. She didn't say much at all. She couldn't. Big chunks of her memory were gone, and most of her words, too. But she wasn't dead, so there was no proof that Glory's father attacked her at all.

And Glory wasn't hurt. Not in any way they could see. We had no proof. She had burned those clothes that he ripped so there was no evidence at all.

The only thing that they proved was that Glory killed her father in cold blood. And all her father had done was to shoot a horse. A mad-crazed horse that had kicked down a barn to attack him. The lawyers said surely you don't kill a man for that.

So Glory's father got a fancy funeral, with everyone making speeches about what a good man he was. Such a loss. So tragic.

Then Violet got sentenced with two years in jail. For horse

thieving, and wounding Glory's father without justifiable cause. Since it was his hand she shot off, the newspapers labeled her a 'man-*hand*-ler'. It was a name sure to dog her the rest of her life, and squash any hope of ever finding true romance.

But the worst thing was Glory. Because Glory was sentenced to hang.

WHEN SHADOWS FALL

- 46 -

We didn't know what to do. We couldn't understand how it had all gone so wrong so fast. Rosey tried to visit Glory in jail, but Glory wouldn't let her come. Glory wouldn't talk to any of the Darlin's.

Until she asked to see me.

I didn't understand it at first. But of course I went.

She didn't want me there for comfort, or support, or any of those things. She wanted a favor. She wanted a rope thin enough to sneak into her jail cell.

But strong enough to do the job herself.

At first I said no. That's not how I wanted it to end.

But she begged me. She begged so hard. She said she paid dear for the right to have no man touch her ever again. It was a price she was willing to pay. But so help her, that price would be wasted if that hangman put his hands on her. She said I had to help her. She said there was no one else who could do it.

She said I couldn't refuse her last request.

I had thought that the bargain I made with Cilla, voting against Lill, would be the worst thing I'd ever be asked to do.

I was wrong.

If it had been anyone else, I would have doubted Glory could actually go through with it.

But this was Glory. The one who rode the bronco, the one whose body broke before her will.

She said, "I know you, Maisy. You're the most honest person I ever met. If you say you will do it, I know that you will. Can you give me that, Maisy? Before you go, can you give me your word you will do this for me?"

I couldn't say it out loud. But I nodded. Just the once. It was enough to seal her fate.

And mine.

She looked away and I left. I went back to the room where the sheriff put me, each of us holed up in a different room so we couldn't "fraternize" and contaminate our accounts of what happened.

As I sat on the slatted bench, feeling the walls close in around me, I started to weave.

It was just a bit of string, really. A length of silk tassel with a core of steel wire.

The next day I brought it to her, hidden in the cuff of my pants. She didn't thank me. I was glad, at least, for that.

"Don't tell," she said.

"Not even Rosey?"

"Especially not Rosey. You can't tell any of the Darlin's."

I didn't understand, but I agreed. I think I would have said anything to get away from that cell.

We said no goodbyes. I just left. There were no words to say what we had exchanged.

I walked out of there completely alone. This was even worse than when I was living off eggs. That was because there was no one else around. But this time, I was alone because I carried a burden I could not share. I knew if I told anyone, they would stop Glory from getting her last wish, that no man would ever take from her again.

There were over 100 executions in America in that year of 1917, a bumper crop for hangings. But of all of them that blood-thirsty year, Glory was the only woman facing a "necktie party." This made her a celebrity. On the day of her hanging, a mountain of people came to see it.

Wrapped up in Papa's barn coat, I stood with the crowd. I

watched as the judge and the lawyers smiled at the throng of people and shook hands, like it was some kind of picnic.

Then the hangman came out. The people went quiet, not out of respect but so they could hear every bit of the sounds to be coming. They were hungry and scared and excited to see the "show."

But they were robbed of it. Because the real hanging had already taken place in the wee hours of night. With Glory all alone in her cell with no friends or strangers, just her iron will.

And my thin little rope.

As I watched with the crowd. I saw the Sheriff's deputy run out to get him, his face all pink and puffy as he pulled the officials aside.

The people got restless. They didn't understand. Then the sheriff explained what had happened. He said there would be no "show," that everyone should just go home.

The people scattered like bugs, bumping and pushing to get away, angry that they'd wasted their time.

I didn't go with them. I refused to leave with that blood-hungry crowd. I didn't have anywhere to go, so I stayed. I remained right where I stood, a defiant reminder that the world would not hang our Glory. We did that ourselves, Glory and me.

I stood there for her, because no one else would.

Hours went by, I suppose, because my legs started to shake.

Rosey and Lill came to get me. Maybe together. Or one at a time. I don't remember how or what they said. I couldn't talk to them. I had promised not to tell so I didn't. I couldn't break a promise that cost Glory her life.

They pulled me away, but I felt nothing. I wasn't quite in their world anymore, but I wasn't in Glory's, either.

I don't know what happened next. All I know is that I didn't move. Wherever they put me, I did nothing, I said nothing. I don't know how long this went on, in the sun, in the dark, in the rain.

Then people in white clothes came and got me. They took me

to a place full of people who no longer belonged.

They poked me and pinched me and asked me all sorts of things. But what could I say? I had talked to Glory, my friend, and that ended up killing her. What words did I have for strangers?

That time in my life is just shadows. Shadows of doctors blending in and out of white walls. Shadows of other people, like me, who were barely there.

Then a familiar shadow came. It was Mama's shadow, leading me off.

I remember shadows of being pushed around pastel rooms with flowers and a cake.

Shadows of a white dress and a church with bells ringing, and a young man with cold eyes.

And a man taking a photograph, a big thing in those days, and my Mama swimming in a sea of faces, all smiling and toasting the day.

I didn't wake up from the shadows until my wedding night, when I found that young man's eyes upon me, no one else in the room. He was doing to me what Glory's father had done to her.

I woke up to that and I screamed for all I was worth. He never touched me like that ever again.

It turns out my new husband was a philandering man. He needed a "pure" wife for his image. My mama traded me to his people for a fine position for herself. She said I wasn't good for much, but at least I had one asset she could bargain off.

Once I "woke" up, I learned all these things. Abner, my new husband, never let me speak of my cowgirling days. If I tried, he'd have me locked away. A sanitarium "rest," he called it. Although it was really so he could go off with his floozies.

He had plenty of those. But none of them ever gave him a child.

No one but me.

Because of that, he wouldn't divorce me. Though there were

many times that I wish that he had. He liked controlling me, the way a mean person breaks in a horse, to boss it around and keep it totally under their will.

He took my son from me and sent him away. I learned to lock away my memories and my thoughts. It was my best defense.

Now he's finally gone, and can't use my past against me. I was hoping it would no longer haunt me, but you can't change what you've been through. At least it can no longer hurt me, and is no more frightening than what the future holds.

True, those cowgirl days were hard work. But it was not all dark and despair back then. And I was not all dark and despairing.

I was something entirely different.

I was alive.

FROM THE ASHES...

- 47 -

I don't know how long I clung to Grandma that day, holding my arms tight around all the little knobs of her spine. I knew that even if I lived to be older than her, I would never meet anyone who had endured more, or triumphed over more than my Grandma Kline.

From that day on, she was a different person. The past no longer clung to her, a tangible presence like stale perfume. She was free of it. And for the third time in her life, she told me, she was happy, thanks to me. According to Grandma, if a person can have three such times in their life, they are three times lucky.

After that, my life felt different, too. I visited her whenever I could, and not just on Fridays. She wasn't broken anymore, and neither was I. We were just two normal people sharing our time, bonded by all the usual things that hold people together -- respect, understanding, and love.

My parents never got why I went. I tried to explain, but it only seemed to make my Dad sad, that he wasn't able to have the same kind of special time with her.

I did bring Sammy along a few times, when he got a little bit older and wasn't such a brat. He didn't know the whole story, just the good parts. He understood that Grandma was special to me, and I think he liked her, too. If he thought maybe Dad was right and she'd made the whole thing up, he never said it out loud. He knew I believed, and he didn't want to take that from me. Imagine that -- Sammy and I getting along.

Grandma and I spent our time well. She didn't need to talk about the past anymore. I'd already heard it. Now she could lay those ghosts to rest. From then on, we talked about all kinds of things, like my parents and teachers, and Miss Belinda's big bushy eyebrows. We talked about the president and movies and books I had read.

I felt bad for my Dad's disappointments in life, but I learned they didn't have to affect me. Life might be hard and crusty, but it was full of hidden pockets of secrets. Secrets that could be mine if I only asked the right questions.

Grandma made me beautiful things. Lace collars, crocheted vests, and a sweater with a big fat tomato embroidered onto the pocket. It was silly but I loved that sweater.

I tried to learn yarn-work from her. I did my best to sew and to knit. But my fingers were clumsy. I stabbed myself with the needles more often than not, and couldn't get the stitches right. I wanted to be like her, but in the way that she was the most special, I was just useless.

I was mad at myself for that. But Grandma told me it was a good thing. She said I was not destined to make her mistakes all over again. She said it warmed her heart to know I was my own person, and would find my calling in my own time.

As close as we were, there was one thing she wouldn't do for me. She would not throw a rope. She said that belonged to another time. Another Maisy who didn't know what was coming, and this one did. This one knew exactly what was coming. What every person has coming, when their body gets old and starts to give out. She said it was nice, for a change, to be just like everyone else.

When the end came, Grandma went fast. One day she started to feel wheezy and two days later, she was gone. That's how she wanted to go, she used to tell me. So of course, that's what she did. People might have thought she was weak, having been married off to a man she didn't know, putting up with his lady friends, and allowing him to treat her like a carton of milk past its shelf life.

But I knew better. She was nobody's fool. Maybe I, alone, in all the world, knew what strength there was in her. That beneath the wrinkles of skin, there was a will of steel wire.

We had her funeral at the big church in town. It was an awfully large room for the tiny handful of people who came. Besides the minister, there was Mom and Dad and Sammy and me, and Miss Belinda from the nursing home.

But I noticed one more person who sat in the back. She was an old woman with a hunch in her back and a gold necklace as thick as a dog collar studded heavy with jewels.

I knew Grandma didn't have friends back in Pittsburgh. She didn't know anybody that rich.

I tried not to think about the old woman in back as the minister delivered his speech, his voice spouting hollow words that echoed against the high ceiling. But I couldn't help but wonder who that mysterious old woman might be.

When the service was over and the minister left, the old woman hobbled up to the front and took my father's hand. I shuffled close to catch every word.

She introduced herself as Mrs. Jonathan Quincy Herringbone. It was a big name, and Father seemed awfully impressed. Then she passed him an envelope. She said it was a scholarship contribution for the deceased's grandchild.

Mother stepped up. "You must have been talking to Samuel's teacher," she said, swelling with pride. "My son is very bright."

"That may be," said the woman. "But he has his own college account, from the sale of the house in Pittsburgh. This is a trust fund for the girl, Anabel. I'd like to speak to her now. Alone, if you please."

My Mom turned three shades of red. But Dad, to his credit, quietly ushered her and Sammy away.

I was left with Mrs. Jonathan Quincy Herringbone all alone,

just the two of us in that big empty church.

"She told you about me, didn't she?" said the woman. "Don't lie to me, girl. I have my sources."

Was she one of grandfather's lady friends?

"Think, girl," she said. "You'll figure it out. You have to be smart or she would never have bothered with you. I knew your grandmother a long time ago, before she was Mrs. Abner Kline. Who am I, Ana Bluebell? Of course you'd have a flower name, too."

My heart lept inside me. She was *one of them!*

"That's right," she said. "I knew Maisy Daisy a long, long time ago. Come on, girl. Which one am I?"

She wasn't tall enough to be Rosey. Or tiny enough for Lill. And she didn't have a trace of Klara's accent.

"Violet?" I whispered.

She shook her head with a sigh. "Your Grandma was the last one left, except for me."

There was only one name left. Could it possibly be...?

She sniffed. "Yes, I'm Priscilla."

I couldn't speak, my words dried up in my mouth.

She said, "She wouldn't have invited me here, that's for certain. But these things aren't for the dead, are they? They're for the living. And that still includes me."

Then she let out a cackle of a laugh, right there in the church, with my grandmother's coffin just a few feet away.

I was so mad I felt sick. The nerve of her. The horrible nerve.

"Come on," she said. "Aren't you least bit curious? Don't you want to know what happened to them?"

Of course I did. But I didn't want to give her that satisfaction. I didn't want to give her a thing.

It must have been my eyes that gave me away.

She smiled, a flash of triumph, and went on. "Rosey went first. Liquor, of course, and a brawl with the wrong crowd. No surprise there. Then Lill threw away her furry pants. Just left them in the dust, and went back to Jackson Hole to work at the bar. She made drinks and cleaned tables. But she couldn't work the cash register anymore. Too much of her thinking was gone. One day, she didn't come in to work. Nobody knows where she went. People looked, but couldn't find a trace. It's like she just disappeared. But in the dark heart of winter when the Jackson windstorms come howling, they say you can see a midnight black horse in the screaming wind with the angel of mercy on his back. A whisp of an angel with big furry pants.

"We never heard from Klara again. Must have changed her name. Who could blame her? She didn't want to go to jail like Violet, who did her time. When they finally let Violet out, she stayed on as the cook, taking care of everyone's stomachs. And oh, how those jailbirds loved her. That's where she found him, her true love. Right there washing dishes in the jail house sink. When his time was up, they bought a sailboat to sail around the world. Free as a pair of birds. Ex-jail birds. You should have seen the send-off they gave that pair. I was there -- I snuck in the back. You've never seen a tribute like it. Not like the speeches and plaques you get from your charity work and donations. This had tears and emotion. The real deal.

"As for me, I had no children, although I married a rich man. Twice! Isn't that the kicker?"

Part of me did want to kick her.

We sat there, two small figures, dwarfed by the soaring arches, with nothing but silence between us.

She fidgeted with her great necklace of jewels, absently sending tiny flashes of color across the tall ivory walls. After a while, she said, "I thought I would feel better. I thought that maybe, if I out-lasted them all, I could finally feel..."

"...Not guilty anymore?" I said.

She frowned. "You've always been hard on me, Maisy."

"I'm not Maisy," I said. "I'm Anabel."

She looked away, as if she was bored. "Oh. Right."

Everything about her made my skin crawl. "If you're trying to buy me off," I said, "you can forget it. Do you think you can give my Dad a check, and pay back what happened?"

"No," she said. For the first time, I saw pain etched into the lines of her face. "I have no illusions of that. Money won't forgive me. I learned that a long time ago. This money is not for me, it's for you, Ana Bluebell. For the last of the Little Darlin's. You ride with it, girl. And don't you ever forget."

RIDE ON

- 48 -

Grandma's will was very short. With her house and her money already gone, all the will listed was her sewing box. She left that to me.

In the bottom compartment, under a skein of tomato red yarn, was a packet of letters and some photos. One picture of Buffalo Bill, signed by the great man himself, read: "To my good friend Tiberius Lee, the best granier in the country." The letters were folded, like they'd been kept in a pocket a long time, and they smelled like corn.

With them was a note from Grandma. It said: "Don't cling to what's gone, the way I did. These papers are worth a lot. Kind of evens things up, don't you think?"

She wanted me to sell them to pay for a college degree. She wanted that kind of chance for me. When I turned 18, that's what I did. I didn't need Cilla's money after all. I worked night jobs and paid the rest of my way through college with the money from Grandma's treasures. I worked hard, not just for Grandma, but for me.

I discovered my Mom was wrong about one thing. People did want a girl who could argue -- especially when they needed a top-notch lawyer. I wish Grandma could have seen where I ended up, but I think she probably knew. She never said it out loud because this was something she wanted me to figure out for myself.

I did my best to avoid her mistakes. I forgave Mom and Dad. Like Dad said, he was just trying to do his best with the cards he'd been dealt.

I even forgave Cilla, despite her blood money. It had to be me to forgive her. As she said, there was no one else left to do it. I figured it was time. After all, we are who we are. Who we were born to be. Mom and Dad. Sammy. And me. And all of the Darlin's.

I will take these stories I know, and tell my daughters. And all of theirs, too. We will run towards our dreams with our hearts, and our legs. We will face our futures with courage and care.

But sometimes we will look back. To see the clear well-spring we came from, that bubbled up from the plains and splashed out across the frontier.

And we will never forget.

- THE END –

ABOUT THE AUTHOR:

Mary Albanese's early cowgirl experiences stemmed from growing up on a small farm in upstate New York, where she was tasked with breaking in the family's horses. After college she moved to Alaska to work as a geological explorer, and became one of the early female geologists in interior Alaska. Her book MIDNIGHT SUN, ARCTIC MOON: MAPPING THE WILD HEART OF ALASKA chronicles her ten years of exploration adventures in the far north.

After that, she traveled around the world with her family, taking on different jobs from radio show host in the Wasatch Mountains of Utah to working as an art therapist in Surrey, England.

Dr. Albanese returns to Alaska every summer to teach art, and currently lives with her family on a farm in the rural core of New Jersey.

www.ingramcontent.com/pod-product-compliance
Lightning Source LLC
Chambersburg PA
CBHW060154180626
46813CB00007B/2745